OUTCAST

(Apocalyptia Book One)

Dedication

As always, this book is dedicated first to my four favorite people, Andi, Aspen, Madison and Sarah, and our newest joy, Miss Zoey. My thanks go out to Jameson for his insightful input, and my amazing critique partners who work so hard to make sense of what I put down on paper. Also, my eternal gratitude goes to my long-ago mentor, Ray Faraday Nelson, who helped me define my world.

Chapter One

apocalyptia: also Apocalyptia, noun.
    1. the period or state of being after the apocalypse;
    2. city on the new coast of California established in
2014

Nicole Mathers bent to grab the bottle of apple-scented shampoo just as California took a nosedive. The shower floor jolted from under her feet and her head slammed against the tile wall. Light flashed behind her eyes and when she squinted through the clear shower curtain, a blurry halo of dust surrounded the ceiling lamp. The floor continued to jump and dance, tossing her about as she reached for a towel and her robe on her way out of the bathroom.

The earthquake showed no signs of stopping. Each dragging second rang with crashes, shattering glass and screams from the neighboring apartments. Her cheap bookshelf fell, the lime green vase on top doing a belly flop before shattering on the carpet.

Unsteady on her feet, Niki waited out the movement,

leg free, or numb?

A wave of panic grabbed at her like an undertow.

She couldn't give in. She was alive, that was all that mattered. That, and getting out of her apartment.

Hoping the lump beneath her was her robe, she lifted her shoulders as far off the carpet as she could in an attempt to free the garment.

She had to get out quickly. Aftershocks could bring down any walls that hadn't already fallen. Her apartment was on the bottom floor of the two-story building. That thought sent waves of nausea through her. If the whole thing was on top of her, how would she escape? Her sister needed to know she was all right. Crystal would wake in her home in Santa Maria in an hour or two to get ready for school and would panic hearing the news of a huge earthquake in Bakersfield.

In the absolute darkness of the pre dawn, Niki couldn't even see her hands. She tried to lift her hips under the weight of the debris, testing how stable the pile was. Nothing moved, so she squirmed to her side. Her left leg was pinned in place.

Reaching down past her hips, she tried to move whatever held her back. No go. Tugging her leg from behind her knee only caused pain where something dug into her ankle.

The only way she was going to get free was if someone dug her out. "Help!"

Silence answered her. People should be screaming, digging out of their apartments, calling for loved ones. Where was everyone? The quiet bothered her the most. Like she was the last person on earth.

Dear God, please don't let me be the only one alive. And don't let me die slowly.

Her stomach growled. She'd kill for a latte. She'd

praying, pleading for it to stop. As quickly as the shaking started, the room settled with one last jolt.

A huge *boom* outside shook her building. Niki's heart jolted. She drew a deep breath and she clutched her robe against her chest. *Clothes. Shoes. Phone.* Her brain shouted orders that her body ignored. She was too frightened to move.

The center of her living room bucked beneath her feet in a second round of quaking. One minute she knew where the front door was, the next, she wasn't sure what room she was in. Her apartment began to shake.

Remembering the advice she'd once seen on the news, she dove to the floor in front of her couch just as the ceiling came crashing down. Tucked up tight in front of the couch, she wrapped her arms over her head and prayed. And prayed.

Stop!

But the floor kept shifting. Chunks of the building fell around her. Dust filled her nose. Moments seemed like hours. She thought it would never end. There wasn't even time for her life to pass before her eyes. Yet it felt like lifetimes passed.

And the earthquake stopped with a fading shimmy.

Dead silence reigned. A spooky lack of the noises of life, broken only by an occasional *chink* of something falling. Weight pressed down on her left leg, digging into her ankle. Niki dared to open her eyes and coughed against the dust that threatened to choke her. Shifting her arms, she lifted her head to survey the damage. Her line of sight was blocked by rubble.

Niki's upper body was in a cavity walled by the couch on one side and a large section of the ceiling angled over her. She couldn't see past her waist, but only felt the heaviness pinning one leg. Was her other kill to see the bitchiest of customers again. Anything, just get her out of this hole. She tried to determine how much time had passed, and noticed weak sunlight slicing through the darkness at her waist. Dawn had come.

And still no one was moving around. "Help, somebody, please. Hello! I'm in here."

A moan sounded from somewhere above her. She couldn't imagine how much rubble might be on top of her.

"Is someone there? I'm Nicole. I live in apartment 101A. I'm stuck."

Somewhere in the distance, a child cried hysterically.

Reaching again for the object pinning her, Niki pushed, rested, pushed and rested. Then pushed again, straining until she thought her head would burst. Suddenly the object shifted. But only an inch or so, not enough to pull her leg free. "Damn it."

Her nostrils were filled with dust, her mouth pasty from panting so much of it in. Her wet hair chilled her skin with the cold morning air. Tears of frustration pooled in her eyes, which made her angry. She never cried. Tears were a waste of energy. Yet a lump burned in her throat, waiting to be cried loose.

She could tell time was passing by the changing shadows made by the wedge of sunlight in her little cave. There was no sound of anyone digging in her building. Was this the end? She was going to die, hungry, naked, trapped in a rundown apartment in the poorest section of Oildale. She had just been promoted to first assistant manager at Taco Shack at the age of eighteen, the youngest person to do so, according to her district supervisor. And she was going to die before she interviewed her first prospective employee. She'd never see her sister again, or get married and have kids. All her dreams were going to wither under a gazillion tons of concrete and two-by-fours.

I don't want to die.

A male voice she didn't recognize called out nearby. "Nicole."

Relief brought the painful lump back in her throat. "I'm here!"

She heard footsteps, debris shifting. Then the voice again. "Say it again. I don't want to walk on top of you."

"I'm here."

Grunts, something heavy sliding, and a thump when it landed. "Keep talking."

"Please, you've got to get me out of here."

His voice sounded tighter. "I'm working on it. Keep your pants on."

Crap. She had no pants to keep on. She was naked, her robe trapped underneath her and who knew where the towel ended up. She squirmed and tugged again at the lump of fabric until she pulled it free, her ankle protesting the movements. Even so, she couldn't put the robe on in the space she had.

The guy was taking forever to move toward her. What was taking him so long? Her skin was frozen. If she could just get warm again…"Can't you hurry?"

"Not if you don't want the rest of the building to fall on us."

"How bad is it? Did the whole thing collapse?" Of course it did, stupid. Where else would all the cement and crap have come from?

"Don't worry about the building, just focus on getting out."

He sounded nearer, and his voice struck a note in her memory. "Do I know you?" she asked.

"I don't know. We both went to North High. I live in Building D."

"What's your name?"

"I'm JC. JC Phillips."

A *thump* of falling debris followed his words and she jumped. She didn't recognize his name, but then she hadn't had a lot of friends in school. "Be careful. It's creepy in here."

He cleared his throat. "Don't expect that to change much when you get out."

More than just her building must have fallen. Once, she'd seen an old newspaper article about a big quake that hit Bakersfield in the '50s, when several of the brick buildings downtown had collapsed. The earthquakes since that one had been smaller. This was the strongest quake she'd ever been through. She thought again about her sister and how worried she'd be. "Do you have a cell phone?"

"Yeah. No signal. I'll bet most of the cell towers are down."

"I need to let my little sister know I'm okay. She'll be worried." Gnawing on her lower lip, she tried to remember where her laptop was. She'd last used it while sitting on the couch. It should have been on the coffee table, and the coffee table was to her left. Or that's where it had been before the shaking started.

She poked at anything she could reach, but it all felt like sticks and stones. Maybe if she had more light, or maybe when JC pulled her out she would better be able to tell what was what.

Near her head, the pile shifted and an avalanche of debris fell, sending her into a coughing fit at the clouds of dust.

"Damn it," JC shouted. "Are you okay?"

She cleared her throat. It felt like she could hawk up a mud ball. "Yeah. What was that?"

"I guess I moved something I shouldn't have. It's kind of hard to tell." He sounded close.

"Where are you? It sounds like you're right above me."

He tapped and she was sure she could reach out and touch him, if she could only see him.

"I'm under here. Please hurry." She pushed at the large cement chunk over her head but it didn't budge.

"I can't hurry. I told you. It's too unstable."

"I know. I'm just getting claustrophobic." Her left leg was growing numb from the weight, and her right arm was asleep.

"Picture yourself somewhere open, like the beach. What beach do you like to go to?"

Visions of sand and water appeared in her mind. "We used to go to Lake Buena Vista when I was a kid and we played on the beach. I didn't see the ocean until I could drive myself there."

"No kidding? But it's so close. My buddies and I used to go to Pismo almost every weekend during the summer. Before I got a job."

Scraping sounded near the end of the couch and she tried to turn her head.

JC grunted and something small fell. "Hey, I think I'm almost there. Can you see my hand?"

"Where?"

"Here." He tapped near where the scraping had been.

She worked her arm above her head and slithered her hand into an opening. Suddenly fingers touched hers. "I feel you," she cried out.

Her sense of urgency doubled. Time froze as she

remained trapped while he continued to move debris and create an opening large enough for her to get through. Finally, sunlight filled her small cave and she saw his face. He reached his arm down to her. "Grab my hand."

She did, and clutched her robe to her chest with the other. As he pulled, she tried to inch toward him, but her leg was still pinned. "I'm stuck. My leg."

"Hang on." His arm disappeared and it seemed hours more passed before the block on her leg moved.

Pain shot through her ankle. She cried out. The weight was gone, and she drew her knees up. Pins and needles pricked at her foot from her blood flowing into it again. "I'm free. I'm coming out now."

Squirming, scraping and listening for the threat of another avalanche, she made her way toward the light. The tunnel seemed endless and JC was nowhere in sight. Panic crept in and took root. She hurried in a combat crawl on her elbows, dragging the rest of her body behind. All the while she kept her robe tucked under one arm.

When she reached the edge of the opening, the sunlight was blinding. She laughed briefly, pulled her legs through and knelt long enough to tug on the robe. "I'm out! I'm alive. JC, where are you?"

"Right behind you, move your ass," he grunted, coming through the hole. He stood, coated in dust, looking like he'd crawled from a flour bin except for the sharp, stark redness of his eyes.

Clutching her robe closed, she threw her free arm over his shoulder and hugged him. "Thank you. My God, thank you."

Embarrassed at her emotional display, she stepped back, cutting her foot on something sharp. She cried out.

JC calmly bent, lifted her foot as if she was a horse, and plucked a bit of metal out. "You need shoes."

"I need clothes." She didn't even have the tie to keep her robe closed.

Standing on the cement walkway outside where her front door should be, reality sank in. Building A, her apartment and eleven others, had been reduced to a pile of unrecognizable rubble. She spun and looked at the other buildings. JC's was also flattened. In fact, only one of the four in the small complex stood partially intact.

She limped out into the grassy common area. Her knees waivered at the realization she had been buried alive, and might have died there if not for JC's help. Glancing back, she saw him standing where she left him, staring blankly after her.

At the next building over, a Hispanic man lay on the grass, reaching into the ruins. His voice was hoarse, as if he'd been screaming a lot. Behind him stood two young children in their pajamas. A baby cried out near another building, pulling Niki's attention away momentarily. When she looked back, the man was alone.

She didn't see where the children had disappeared to. The more she looked around the small complex, the heavier the feeling of helplessness became. She didn't know where to start, who she could help. Who was beyond help.

Suddenly she remembered hearing moans from within her building. She returned to the mess that had been her building, where JC still stood. "Someone else is trapped."

"You have a roommate?"

"No. One of my neighbors. I heard someone moaning." She struggled to remember what direction the sound had come from. "Down that way."

They skirted the building, and Niki looked for anything resembling a human in the pile of plaster and broken furniture. "The bedrooms are all at the inside. I can't walk over all that."

Her feet felt like ice cubes. Glancing down, she saw pink toes at the end of feet coated in white powder. She probably was covered in the dust, her hair now cement dreadlocks. While JC climbed awkwardly on shifting rubble, she bent and looked into crevices. She found the corner of a door and lifted with her free hand. A pair of bare feet appeared. "Over here."

JC scrambled toward her, slipping once when a table collapsed under him. "Step back."

She did, wrapping her arms around herself while she waited.

He lifted the door higher, shouldering it as he bent toward the man. Niki peered around him. A dark pool of dried blood circled the man's head, but before Niki could see more, JC straightened and lowered the door carefully. He took her shoulder and steered her away. "It's too late."

Nausea cramped her stomach. She tugged free of JC's grip. An urgent need to talk to her boss, Lisa, hit hard. She was the closest thing Niki had to a mother. But JC said there was no signal on his phone. The Taco Shack where she'd worked up until her promotion last week was only a few miles away, much closer than Lisa's house. Someone would be there. Anne, who took over her shifts, should be overseeing the preparations for opening. With luck, the phones there would be working and she could call Lisa and Crystal.

JC stopped beside her. His jeans hung low the way the gang-bangers wore theirs, his graphic t-shirt baggy and hanging untucked beneath his thick hoodie. His gray beanie slouched toward the back of his head. He must work the early shift at his job, to have been fully dressed when the earthquake hit, although what kind of job he was dressed for, she couldn't say. "Hey, Mouse—"

"Don't call me Mouse." In a flash, she remembered who he was. Old memories of hateful teasing came crashing down on her, bringing back the pain of being so far outside the accepted crowd in high school. In their minds she was a rodent, eating trash and living in filth. She'd survived by fighting back with more name-calling, which hadn't made her any friends.

His use of that nickname showed how far apart they were. She was an assistant manager of a new Taco Shack and he was stuck in high school in his head. His clothes spelled out who he was. *Loser.*

Inwardly, she cringed. *Snark much, Niki? That loser just saved your life.* "Thank you for pulling me out of there. No one would have come looking for me, except maybe my boss."

"I was worried about you. Thought you might be hurt."

He was worried about her. That surprised her. She hadn't thought about him, ever, that she could remember, although she'd noticed him around the apartment complex. They'd spoken maybe twice in the six months since they graduated, and not much more than that in the year she attended North High with him. He and his "bros" had been random faces passing in the hallways, making smartass remarks at the geeks she hung out with. "I need to find a phone and call Crystal. And my boss. Lisa will be worried if I don't show up for work."

He glanced at the slow motion, unearthly quiet

chaos around them. "I don't think anyone's showing up for work today, Mouse."

Chapter Two

Standing close in the bright sunlight, Niki saw JC's face, pale beneath the dust, his eyes rimmed in red as if he'd been up all night. Or was high. He didn't act as if he was tweaking or stoned, but in their neighborhood, you never knew.

A breeze kicked up sending shivers across her skin. She suddenly remembered she had a spare uniform and a pair of shoes in the trunk of her car, for those times she was called into work when someone didn't show up. She headed for the parking lot of the apartment complex.

"Be careful," JC warned, hurrying to catch up with her. "You'll cut your feet again."

Her ankle throbbed with each step. She had no choice but to walk barefoot, if she wanted to reach her shoes, and she ignored the pokes and pinches of the gravel beneath her feet. Ignored the footsteps telling her JC followed. "I'll be fine. You can go back to your mom and sister now. I've got clothes in my car and I'll go find my boss. Her house is probably fine and I can crash there for now."

Damn. She stopped short. "I don't have my keys." Her keys were in her purse, and her purse was under two apartments' worth of concrete and plaster. She wasn't driving anywhere anytime soon. Neither was she opening her trunk where her clothes were. Deciding to break a window if she had to, she continued around the van parked near the walkway.

Her ancient Chevy was directly behind the van. And directly under a lamppost. It had toppled across her trunk. She couldn't win. "No," she whined as she got close. "My poor car."

With one hand clutching her robe closed, she wrestled the lamppost off the trunk and circled her car, trying the door handles on the odd chance she'd left one unlocked.

No luck.

"Do you have a hide-a-key?" JC asked.

"No. I don't even have a spare. I bought the car used."

"I can help," he said in quiet monotone and walked away.

She shook her head, watching him disappear around the van. His robotic, flat emotions were probably due to the shock of the quake. People reacted differently to emergencies. She became hyper, frantic and energetic to fix the problem. He apparently shut down emotionally.

Standing alone gave her time to notice how cold the morning air was and how undressed she still was. The soles of her feet stung on the chilly pavement. Her left shin had a massive bruise, and the scrape on her ankle was crusting over. Maybe when she got to Lisa's she could shower again. And borrow some underwear. She only had pants, a blouse and her awful black safety-soled shoes in the car.

Looking toward the street, she wondered where the emergency vehicles were. The sun was midway in the sky, so where was help? She didn't even hear sirens in the distance. There should be rescue crews rushing in to save survivors. Ambulances taking victims to the hospital. The Sheriff's Department should have squad cars patrolling the damage and helping where they could. But no one drove on the streets, as if the city itself was in shock.

Or everyone was dead.

Chimneys of black smoke dotted the horizon where buildings burned. Most were thin and scattered, but a huge cloud hung over the edge of Oildale where the oilfields were.

JC returned and silently went to work breaking into her car with a piece of scrap metal. Once he had the door open, he popped the trunk latch from the dashboard button. She used the open trunk lid as a shield to dress behind. The cold fabric brought her skin temperature down even more. Shivering, she yanked the bathrobe on over her clothes and slid her feet into her shoes.

Suddenly her car's engine purred to life. She walked to the driver's door where JC's legs stuck out. "How did you do that?"

He sat up from beneath the dash, his face expressionless. "Just something I learned in auto shop."

"They don't teach you how to hotwire cars in auto shop. Do they?" Stupid question. Of course they didn't.

He climbed out of the car and she got behind the wheel. "I guess I owe you thanks again. I'm, uh, gonna go find Lisa. Then go see my sister in Santa Maria. I'll see you around. I guess."

He didn't move, so she couldn't shut the door. His eyes stayed locked on her. "You shouldn't go."

Motioning toward the complex, she said, "My apartment is gone. There's nothing to stay here for."

He glanced over his shoulder at the street. "It's not safe out there. Power's off all over. I talked to some deputies this morning. They said there were quakes all over the state. It's not safe to travel in town, much less all the way to Santa Maria."

Her hands loosened their grasp on the steering wheel as her gut dropped. "Were there any earthquakes on the coast? Is…is Santa Maria okay?"

"I don't know. They didn't say how bad it hit in any certain spot. But still…the roads…they might be broken up. And people will be going crazy, who knows, maybe shooting and robbing. You can't go alone."

"I have to see my sister." With renewed determination, she grabbed the armrest on her door. "JC, move, please. I need to get going."

He stayed put. "Mouse, it's not safe out there. It's not safe anywhere right now, but you should stay here where your friends can watch out for you. Where I can watch out for you. At least until they say it's safe to travel."

What the freak? He'd never been a friend. And right now, he was a little creepy following her around. She wasted time talking to him when she needed to be with Crystal. What if her sister needed her? She leaned into the opening to look up at him. "Look, I know you have family here. Why don't you go take care of them? I'll be fine now."

JC's jaw tightened. His face went white, then red. Niki sat back quickly, uncertain what he would do. Was he a tweaker? Was he high on meth? God, why did he have to pick on her? She'd thanked him already, he should leave.

His head dropped and he took a loud breath, his

shoulders shaking. Niki waited, unable to do anything else. Finally, he lifted his head and pierced her with the pain in his eyes.

Realization hit hard, knocking her breathless. She swallowed a lump that settled in her stomach like lead. His family was dead. She couldn't bear thinking of the pain he must be suffering. "Oh, God, I'm so sorry," she whispered.

"I wasn't home. I couldn't help them, got there too late." His voice cracked. "I should've been there."

Moisture pooled in his eyes. Niki wanted to hurl. Instead, she took a deep breath. "Don't you need to do something, take care of whatever? Make arrangements?"

He let go of the car door, straightening and shoving his hands in his front pockets. "There's nothing I can do for them now. But I can watch out for you. If you're going to Santa Maria, I'm going with you."

She watched his face as a million emotions passed over it. Guilt plagued her. On the one hand, he'd saved her life. On the other, she didn't really know this guy, and what she did know of him wasn't anything she'd look for on a job application. More likely, she'd toss his application in the *not if he were the last guy in Bako* pile. But he was alone now. Just like she was. Like she'd been for years. She knew what that hollowness felt like, how it threatened to swallow you like quicksand. She had no idea what the road conditions were between Bakersfield and Santa Maria. If things were as bad as he said, it'd probably be nice to have some muscle on her side. Not that he appeared to have much muscle on that lanky frame.

"Come with me." As she nodded to him and waited for him to get in the passenger side, she wondered who was saving whom.

~*~

JC buckled his seatbelt automatically, although he couldn't care less at this point if he died. He was cold, achingly cold. If he weren't so numb, his bones would hurt. He'd had a headache when he first woke up but that had faded by the time he'd reached the apartment complex.

He was such a loser. No, worse. He couldn't even think of a word to describe what he was. All the swear words he knew didn't come close.

If he hadn't gotten drunk last night, his mom and sister would be alive. It was that simple. There were no take-backs with death. No do-overs. No, *I promise Mom, I'll be good next time.* There were no more levels to play to earn another chance. Game over.

He couldn't even feel good about rescuing Mouse. As much as he thanked God he'd gotten to her in time, it wasn't enough. If he spent the rest of his life trying to help people, it would never be enough.

Shit, he had to quit calling her Mouse. He hadn't learned her real name until months after his friends had started teasing her. He should've stood up to those losers, or made better friends, but he wasn't good at that. Standing up or making friends.

He liked to think of her as Mouse, though. It suited her. Small. Innocent. He'd had a pet mouse when he was a kid and it used to sit on his shoulder everywhere he went. He wished he'd tried to make friend with Mouse, no, Niki, back in school.

He wished he'd done a lot of things differently. But mostly he wished he'd come home last night.

~*~

The desolate scenery didn't change as Niki drove out

of their neighborhood. Most of the tiny houses, built before World War II, were now piles of sticks. Small groups of people huddled together up and down the streets. Trees were uprooted, lampposts leaned at crazy angles or were completely toppled. The traffic signals were out, some blinking red, some completely blank, and the few cars on the road moved cautiously through the intersections.

Brick buildings in the older stretch of Chester Avenue had walls missing. Plate glass windows were shattered, but no one ran in and out of the businesses, stealing everything they could get their hands on. On one block she smelled gas, and she sped up to get away from the area as quickly as she could.

Approaching the local fire station, she saw part of the reason for the lack of emergency vehicles. The firefighters were digging their trucks out from the brick building. The front corner of the station had collapsed on top of the trucks.

Niki shivered as she drove, not from cold but from nerves. She turned up the car heater a notch. Cars around them moved in slow motion. Everything seemed to happen in slo-mo, and she didn't think it was only her perception. The damage to homes and businesses was massive, the surreal stillness reminding her of a tour at Universal Studios. Any minute she expected to see zombies stagger from an alleyway and one of those cameras on wheels roll past.

Only three cars were in the parking lot at the Taco Shack. The back half of the building had crumbled like stale cookies. A few feet from the rubble, a body lay under a trashcan liner. Several people huddled near the dumpster. Niki jumped from her car as soon as it stopped.

She recognized the restaurant owner among the bystanders. Dread filled her at the thought of who lay beneath the black plastic. "Pete, is everyone okay?"

Everyone turned. Pete motioned toward the body. "Afraid not. We lost one."

"Wh—who is it?"

"Anne Keller."

No, it couldn't be. Not Anne. Niki's stomach lurched. "She's dead?" The words had to be forced past the lump in her throat.

"Yeah," Pete said. He was pale, his eyes wide and glassy. "She was at her desk when the wall fell on her. The other two kids got out okay. I sent them home. I'm waiting till someone comes to claim the body."

The body. Niki wanted to scream, *That's not a body, that's Anne!* but she bit her lower lip. She tried to get her mind around the fact the form under the trash bag was her friend. Anne had taken over Niki's shift last week, when Niki got promoted. It could have been Niki there, under the trashcan liner. Dead. She blinked and saw Anne standing there in her jeans and frilly pink flowered shirt, her hair hanging free, looking like she did during managers' meetings on her days off. When Niki blinked again, she was gone.

Without warning, her stomach heaved and she wretched. She ran a couple of steps, bent and vomited up bile. When the queasiness finally passed, she wiped her chin and moved away from the smell. She caught the sympathy in Pete's gaze. "How big was the quake?"

"I heard 8.9," said one of the strangers.

"Nah, it's gotta be bigger. Someone said it was ten-something," said another. They continued to talk about what buildings had fallen, and what others had to say about it. "I don't know where they're getting their figures, since I can't pick up any TV or radio."

"Does anyone have a working phone?" Niki asked.

The answer was a unanimous no. One man added, "Cell towers are down. Electricity is out almost everywhere. Some of the older landlines with a cord might be working but the phone lines are down all over. No telling if your call would go through."

Niki looked at the rubble and the place where the phone was, the manager's desk. Where Anne had been sitting when the walls caved in on her. She couldn't do it. Couldn't go see if the phone worked. Couldn't face the reminder that she could easily be dead. She glanced at JC who stood silently on the edge of the group, and turned back to Pete. "I'm going to go find Lisa. I'll tell her about Anne."

"She's already been by here, said she would look for you."

"She didn't come to my apartment. I guess I'll go by her house."

Pete nodded, and then turned back to what the other men were saying. With a glance toward her coworker's body, Niki fought back another wave of nausea. Signaling to JC, she headed back to her car. Out of habit, reached for the cell phone in her pocket before remembering it wasn't there.

Fresno and L.A. were only a couple of hours away, so she couldn't understand why there weren't power company trucks prowling the streets. Visalia was closer, but they might have had earthquake damage too, as bad as it was. She only saw one or two utilities trucks as she drove, and no emergency vehicles. Again she thought about movies and zombies and—

Wait a minute. Christmas was four days away. "No freakin' way!"

"What?" JC asked.

"Today's December 21st, isn't it? All anyone's been talking about for the last few years is how the Mayans said the world would end on December 21, 2012. Just how big was this earthquake? How far-spread?"

"That's crazy. I dunno."

All her life she'd heard about epicenters and fault lines. It was a part of being a Californian. Earthquakes happened in one location, along one fault line, and rippled outward like when a pebble fell into water. She guessed the San Andreas Fault had shifted, so they could have had quakes anywhere from San Francisco to San Bernardino. Just because it hit Bakersfield so hard didn't mean it was this bad elsewhere. It was a coincidence, not the end of the world.

The image of Anne's black work shoes poking out from under the black trash bag filled her head. It had been the end of the world for some people.

Crystal, why the hell are you so far away? I need to talk to you. She stole a glance at JC, who stared out the side window. "You don't think this had to do with the Mayan thing, do you?"

He didn't look at her. "Does it matter?"

"I don't know. Yeah. It will tell me how big this is. Is California falling into the ocean? When I come through the pass at Santa Maria, am I going to see land or water? Is this the end of the world?"

JC shrugged. Niki hoped he wasn't going into shock at the destruction around them, at the destruction of his family. JC couldn't go into shock. As much as she didn't want to admit it, she needed him. They needed each other. This mess was a lot bigger than she had ever seen.

Aftershocks continued to rattle the city. More

people gathered in clusters on the streets. Nowhere to go. No way to get help when the whole city needed it at once. Since the earthquake hit so early in the morning, no one would have been in the few tall office buildings downtown, and the single- and two-story houses would make rescue and recovery easier. Once they dug the living out of the rubble there was nothing to do but wait. Wait for someone to tell them what happened next.

Niki couldn't wait. After she checked in with Lisa, she would drive to Santa Maria and find Crystal. Maybe she could crash on her sister's couch, if Crystal's adoptive parents would let her. Maybe she would look for a job there, to be close to her sister again. This could end up in her favor. Her thoughts raced ahead with plans, trying to search for normalcy.

She jerked the steering wheel, crossing two lanes of traffic to make a right turn. No one honked, no one hit her, so she must have been the only car around. She didn't know. She couldn't focus. She shouldn't be driving, but what else could she do? A sudden need for normalcy made her want to see the new Taco Shack, the one she was supposed to be at that morning, interviewing potential hires.

The new strip mall had been completed a month ago and it was a mess. Glass all over the walkways in front of the empty shops. The walls and roofs stood, a testament to building codes. *If only Anne could have been working at this store.*

The area was deserted. Niki parked and got out of her car, shading her eyes from the sunlight as she scanned the streets in both directions. She pulled her bathrobe tighter over her clothes for warmth. The businesses across the street had varying degrees of damage. The houses farther down reminded her of pictures of tornado damage, some standing, most not.

Niki shivered, feeling once again like the last person on earth. *Don't be silly.* JC walked up to stand beside her, his shoulders hunched, fists in his pockets, a reminder she wasn't alone.

Suddenly Anne stood before her in that same pink flowered shirt with the ruffled v-neck collar. She raised a hand to Niki but said nothing. She looked sad. Lost.

Niki grabbed JC's sleeve. "Do you see that?"

"See what?"

"Anne."

"Who's Anne?" He turned to look behind them, obviously not seeing the ghost. Anne vanished.

The sound of tires on pavement called Niki's attention. Lisa pulled up, blocking Niki's car, and she jumped out with her engine running. "Thank God, you're all right!"

Peace filled Niki as her boss enveloped her in a hug. Lisa was the mother she wished she'd had, the person who had given her direction and helped her get her act together. Niki held onto her as if her life depended on it.

"Anne," she said into Lisa's shoulder. "Anne's…"

Lisa stroked the back of her head. "I know, sweetie. I went by there. I'm on my way to talk to her family but I had to be sure you were okay. I saw your apartment building and thought we'd lost you, too. I wanted to call, but the stupid phones—"

"I know, I can't call Crystal and tell her I'm okay."

"Why don't you drive there? Do you have enough gas?" Lisa stepped back, holding both of Niki's hands.

"Yeah, I filled the tank two days ago and have only driven to work and back. I wanted to see if I could help, if you needed me…"

Lisa's smile reassured her. "I don't think we're going

to be holding interviews for a few days. Maybe months, the way the town looks. There's no point in staying here. Pete will need to visit all six of his stores and see what shape they're in before deciding on repairs. He'll probably reassign people to fill this one. You need to let your sister know you're okay. Go."

Niki squeezed her boss's hands. "I'd better get moving before the roads get crowded. It's weird having no one driving around."

Lisa nodded, then looked at JC, holding out her right hand as if it was any normal working day. "I'm Lisa."

He shook her hand. Niki introduced him to her boss. "JC pulled me out from under my apartment building."

"My God, are you okay?" She held Niki at arms' length, looking her over. "Why are you wearing your bathrobe?"

"I'm okay. Bruised and stuff but I'll be fine. I was in the shower when it hit and didn't have time to find clothes, or my coat. Luckily, I had these in the car. So, um, JC's gonna ride along with me to Santa Maria."

The look her boss gave her warned her that she'd have to spill all the details of her relationship with JC the next time they met. Too bad there was nothing to say. *He's just some loser I went to school with who saved my life. Now I don't know what to do with him.* Awkward.

"I'd better get going." Niki stepped away and walked to her car, glancing over her shoulder at Lisa. She had this creepy feeling it might be the last time she saw her boss. She fought the urge to go grab one last hug. It was not the end of the world. It wasn't!

"Wait," Lisa called. "Take my coat. You'll need it. I have others at the house."

"Yes, Mother." Laughing, Niki pulled off her robe and put on the coat, still warm from Lisa's body. Then she grabbed that last hug and got in her car.

Chapter Three

Niki made her way back to the main streets, trying to decide which direction to head once she got out of town. There were three main routes to the coast from Bakersfield. One took Highway 46 to Pismo, one took a tiny highway through Taft to Santa Maria, and the other meant driving an hour toward L.A. and taking the 128 through Fillmore and Santa Paula.

JC stretched back in his seat. As if reading her mind, he asked, "Which route are you taking?"

"I guess the 46."

"I wouldn't." He reached forward and pushed the buttons on the stereo. Varying levels of static rang through the speakers. "Wow, this thing is old. Cassettes, huh? No stations are working. You'd think some would have a generator so they could broadcast emergency info."

"Try AM," she said, coming to a stop at a major intersection. "And what's wrong with the 46?"

"It's the one everyone will head toward. Let's take the back roads."

"Won't the roads be messed up?" She drove under

the speed limit, weaving around debris in the streets. Larger objects like the signal poles had been dragged to the curbs, but piles of bricks and downed trees of various sizes littered the way. More cars were on the road now.

"Asphalt's asphalt. Both routes will be a mess, most likely. The shoulders will be wide enough on the back roads for us to get around."

She bit her lip. She didn't like his use of "we" and "us". Yeah, he rode in her car but that didn't make them a "we" in any form. They were two separate people, him and her, driver and passenger. But she didn't want to be a bitch, not when he'd just lost his family.

Not when he'd just saved her life.

Drawing in a shaky breath, she wondered how he could walk away from his home like that. He had a real family. He should try to let his grandparents or someone know about the deaths of his mom and sister. Start planning the funerals. Instead, he insisted on coming with her to find Crystal. It didn't make sense. She stole a glance at him. He stared straight ahead, his eyes squinted against the bright sunlight. Thank God the tule fog that often settled in at that time of year was nowhere around.

JC's beanie hid his hair, but she remembered it as short, almost as short as military guys wore. He had thin, dark eyebrows, and she thought his eyes were brown, but hadn't ever really paid attention. Or stood close enough to tell. His hand lay limp in his lap. Some sort of small symbols or letter were tattooed on the knuckles. She could only see the palm of the other hand, so she wasn't sure if they continued there. What did it say?

Probably something crude and unimaginative, she decided, then bit back the thought. She really wasn't giving him a chance. She didn't usually feel this bitchy. She needed something to eat. And her nerves were on edge. If Crystal had been through an earthquake like the one that hit Bakersfield, she could be going crazy wondering if Niki was okay. At least Crystal had her parents to take care of her.

At one time, both sisters had lived with the Farmers, but Niki had done her best to ruin any shot she ever had of being loved. It embarrassed her to think about the way she had acted, the stunts she pulled. The Farmers tried, really tried, to work with her to fit in, but she only fought harder.

An ancient pickup truck, primer gray, pulled out of a side street directly in her path. Niki jerked the wheel toward the curb, then swerved to miss the tree lying there. Her car bumped and scraped over the upper branches. "Damn it! What are they doing?"

JC held onto the "oh shit" handle above his door. "Crazy-ass drivers are going to be even crazier now with signals out, stop signs down. You're doing good to go slowly."

She bit back a sarcastic remark about her ability to handle herself in an emergency and took a deep breath. She acted like she was PMSing, with her acid thoughts. *Give the guy a chance to prove he's an ass before calling him on it. Geez.*

She needed to make nice. What did you say to someone who's probably in shock, mourning? There had to be a safe subject to talk about. "So, where do you work?"

"Body Elite. The gym."

"Oh, wow, like, as a trainer?"

He gave her an odd look at her surprise. "Yeah."

"How'd you end up doing that?"

"I dunno. I liked gym class, so I signed up for more classes at BC."

Huh. So much for him being the loser. He went on to community college after graduation, while she'd kept working in fast food. "That's cool. I didn't know."

"I heard you were going to manage that new Taco Shack."

"Yeah. Did you let your boss know you're leaving town?"

"You're kidding, right? Who's gonna go to the gym at a time like this?" He sank lower in the seat, looking slightly more comfortable. "Who's gonna notice I'm not around?"

"I'll let you lift the big crap out of the road if we can't get through somewhere. We can't let you get out of shape." She almost smiled as she teased him.

"No problem."

At the rate they were traveling, it would be a couple of hours before they even left Bakersfield city limits. She had chosen one of the main streets west, but should probably have gone north to Seventh Standard Road and avoided the populated areas completely. The industrial area known as Fruitvale didn't have any tall buildings, thank goodness, because the buildings had crumbled. Single story ones didn't make as big a mess. Welding trucks, pickup trucks and a few passenger cars scattered the divided four-lane road, some crashed, some abandoned for no apparent reason. Most of the traffic was going back toward town as if the oilfield workers had been caught in the field when the quake hit, and were headed home to check on their families.

As they approached a convenience store in the midst of the businesses, traffic came to a stop. Cars from both westbound lanes waited to pull into the tiny parking lot or up to the two fuel pumps on one side of the building. A hand-scrawled sign read "NO GAS", but people were arguing outside the store. "Idiots. The pumps don't work without power. Nor do the cash registers."

JC nodded. "We're going to see a lot of this."

Niki noticed his eyes were less red. Maybe it was a good thing she let him come along. Still, she felt odd sitting next to him in her car. And now they were stuck in traffic, blocked on three sides by cars and trucks, and on the other side by a chain link fence. "At this rate it'll be next week before we get to the coast."

He met her gaze. "Nah. Once we get moving, take Coffee up to Seventh Standard and there'll only be a mile or so of businesses before we're clear. We should be able to make up time on the open roads."

As they sat in place, Niki felt the car begin to sway slightly, then jump, then rock big time. She clutched the steering wheel. "Aftershock."

JC ducked his head to look toward the sky, twisting to scan the area on all sides. "We're good. No power poles or trees around to fall on us."

She couldn't speak as long as her car rocked. How could he be so calm? It felt like fifteen minutes passed before the movement stopped, but she knew it was only seconds. Her heart took even longer to calm down, and her grip hadn't loosened on the wheel. "How come you're not scared like I am?"

His face showed no emotion when he answered. "We're safe in the car. It's not like the road is going to swallow us."

"How can you be sure? I mean, I never imagined my shower walls would rear up and attack me, so how do I know what the road will do? I've seen pictures where sink holes open up. Bridges drop. Back in '94, the Northridge quake, that CHP motorcycle cop was killed when the freeway overpass collapsed under him."

JC's hand covered hers on the steering wheel, imparting a small bit of warmth as he wrapped his fingers around hers. "We're gonna be okay, Mouse."

She turned her head. He didn't smile. His eyes pierced into her, almost demanding she believe. "Okay."

Taking another deep breath, she repeated, "Okay. You're right. We're going to be okay. Crystal's okay and we're going to find her."

Her words had barely faded when the sound of tires screaming filled the air. Niki jumped in her seat, twisting to see where it came from. It sounded like one long burnout, tires moving in one place. White smoke billowed around the car behind them, overtook their car and swallowed them up. Her car jolted, hit from behind. It jerked again.

"What the freak?" she screamed.

~*~

JC unbuckled, ready to go after whoever was trying to wreck them. Adrenaline filled his arms and legs. "Somebody's tired of waiting. There's too much smoke, but it looks like a four-wheeler is trying to drive over the guy behind us."

Niki's car jumped again. "That's crazy. I'm gonna hit the guy in front of us."

As she said it, they were pushed into the car's bumper, crunching metal and grinding brake pads battling with her shrieks. "Stop, stop, stop!"

JC threw open his door and jumped out into the thinning smoke. He slammed the heel of his hand against the hood of the big truck. "Knock that shit off," he yelled.

A couple of other guys came up behind him, yelling at the driver. JC pointed at the cars around them. "Can't you see we're blocked in, too? Nobody can get out of your way no matter how badly you want it."

Walking to the car in the next lane beside the truck, JC bent down and talked to the driver, who steered his car up the island curb and onto the wrong side of the road. The truck followed and burned rubber down the island.

JC and the other guys cheered and fist-bumped each other, then they returned to their cars. A tall, skinny black guy stood on the side of the road, watching him. JC recognized an old friend. "What's up?"

Antwon grinned. "Nothin' much, man. Just hangin'."

JC walked over to the curb. "This is a weird place to hang out."

With a cockeyed grin, Antwon said, "Good as any. Gas line ruptured at my uncle's place and we had to leave. I didn't want to go to my aunt's mom's house. They got too many kids there, the place is crazy with noise. So I walked down to the highway to see what was happenin'."

"Do you have anywhere to go?"

He stared off toward the city. "Don't think they'll be having classes for a while. No one's gonna miss me."

JC knew the emptiness of those words. "Want to hang with us?"

"May as well."

Most of the cars behind Niki's had taken the "high road" of escape, clearing the logjam behind them. They could get moving again. JC opened the passenger door and leaned down. "Hey, I found a buddy of mine. This here's Antwon."

Antwon bent down and grinned. "Hey."

Niki said hello, and looked at JC like she was ready to go. He held his breath as he asked, "Okay if he rides along?"

"Well, I guess." Her lips thinned and her eye lids narrowed. "I don't know where we're going to stay or how we'll eat, but why not?"

JC sighed with relief and tipped the front seat forward. Antwon folded himself into the back seat, his legs on one side and his body on the other. JC hopped in, slid the passenger seat farther forward and looked at Niki. She didn't seem pissed off, but he didn't know her well enough to be sure.

Pointing to the center island, he said, "See if you can move into the other lane there and we'll get going."

It took a couple of tries before she gave the engine enough gas to get the first wheel up the curb, but they were rolling again. Antwon leaned an arm on JC's seat back. "So, where we headed?"

"Santa Maria," JC said. "Niki's got a sister there."

"Cool. I've never seen the ocean."

JC didn't have the heart to tell him they weren't going to the shore. To be honest, he had no idea what would happen once Niki found Crystal. She would probably want to stay with her sister, but wouldn't want him and Antwon around. They'd have to hitch a ride back to Bako.

Or move on. He had no reason to go back, now that Mom and Kaylee were gone.

Kaylee's laughter rang out so clearly he looked to see if the others heard it. Neither one reacted. She laughed again, in his head, and a giant fist grabbed his heart and squeezed. How was he going to live without her?

And Mom. The only person besides Kaylee who ever loved him. He hadn't even told her he wasn't coming home last night.

He had to stop thinking about it before he puked. He had to let them go. Focus on getting Niki to Santa Maria safely and see what came up after that.

Chapter Four

An hour later, after detours and roadblocks, and one backtrack and reroute, they were on the outskirts of the city. Niki heard an odd noise from under the hood. "Oh, no," she moaned. As if she hadn't filled her bad stuff quota for the day. Steam rose around the hood of the car. She pulled to the side where there were no trees and asked JC to disconnect the wires and turn off the motor. After he did so, the guys hopped out.

"Pop the hood," JC said. She did. Eventually, he came to her door and opened it. "It's not good. The radiator got cracked when we hit the bumper of that other car."

"What can we do? I can't wait to have it fixed. I need to get to Crystal."

JC looked down the road. "We can try hitchhiking, maybe someone will give us a ride. We can walk while we wait."

Walk. To Santa Maria. They had at least a hundred freakin' miles left to go. But she didn't have enough money to fix her car even if they found a place open for service. Her choices were pretty simple. Sit in the car and hope the radiator fixed itself, or walk. She unbuckled her seatbelt and got out, smothering an urge to kick her tire.

She remembered seeing something when she'd gotten dressed in the parking lot. "Hey, I have coolant in the trunk. Will that help?"

"It'll be cold, so we have to wait until the engine cools to add it. But it might get us to Santa Maria where maybe we can find a repair shop."

Niki got back in the car to wait. The guys stayed out on the side of the road, talking, tossing pebbles into the weeds and being guys. She wished she could talk to her sister. Or better yet, wished she could go back to bed and start the day over. Skip the whole earthquake thing, and the road trip with two guys she knew nothing about.

Her entire day sounded like the opening lines of one of those reality talk shows. *Nicole Mathers thought she'd be starting her new job that Friday, but that was before The Earthquake.* In years to come, she would always think of the event in capital letters, like The Depression and the War in Iraq. Some things divide your life into Before and After. Having your apartment building fall down on top of you was one of those events.

The sound of her passenger door opening woke her, and Niki realized she'd fallen asleep. JC reached into the glove compartment and popped the trunk release. Her stomach growled as she watched him retrieve the coolant and stick his head under the hood. She was hungry. And tired. She said a quick prayer that the road to Santa Maria was clear of traffic and not blocked by fallen trees or power lines.

Antwon stuck his head in the passenger side. "You got any gum?"

"Gum?"

"Yeah. We need some."

She automatically reached onto the floor on the passenger side to grab her purse, then remembered she didn't have it. Instead she opened the glove box and pulled out her insurance and registration papers, some fast food napkins, and a small box of tampons. She cringed and tucked that under the front seat. From the bottom of the space she pulled out an old pack of gum with a few pieces in it. "Cinnamon okay?"

"Yeah, sure." Antwon took the gum and disappeared behind the car hood.

Niki was curious and climbed out of the car. The guys were chewing madly. Antwon handed his piece to JC, who balled the two together.

"This'll do it." JC bent over the engine and reached inside. Then poured the bottle of coolant into the radiator. He straightened and told her, "Start it up."

"I don't have the key."

He ducked his head and walked around the car. "I forgot."

The engine jumped to life. He walked back to her. "Cool. I guess we got it cooled down before the engine block cracked."

"What's with the gum?"

"I stuck it on the crack. It'll slow the leak. Ready to go?" He reached for the support bar to lower the hood.

"Wait, the radiator cap." Niki grabbed the cap from on top of the air cleaner and began to put it where it belonged.

"No, we need it off. The pressure of the closed system will blow the gum off."

The what? She stared at JC. There was a lot more going on in his head than she'd ever have guessed. "Okay. Whatever." She handed him the cap and got back in the driver's seat.

As soon as the guys were seated, she pulled out on the road again. It struck her that she hadn't seen any cars passing by. If it weren't for JC and Antwon, she'd feel like the world ended and everyone forgot to tell her.

Passing through the tiny town of Dustin Acres, she saw families camped out in front of their houses. Less than ten miles farther through the barren hills, they reached Taft where the scene was similar.

Antwon leaned forward and braced his arms on the front seats. "We should see if we can get some water or something. For us and the car. I'm getting hungry."

"Yeah, me, too." JC pointed up ahead. "Pull into the shopping center. Let's see if we can get anything at the market."

The shopping center was chaotic. A pair of sheriff's cars blocked the grocery store entrance doors and the two deputies stood by with rifles in hand. People were lined up waiting to reach the tables where water and bread and some canned goods were stacked.

Niki parked the car. "You guys want to get what you can? I'll wait in the car since I can't shut it off."

"It'll overheat, sitting here," JC said. "We'd better turn it off and let it cool. We can add more water before we go."

By the time they left Taft the sun was setting, but they had granola bars and bottled water. Niki felt a little more human after eating and drinking.

It still seemed odd that no one else travelled the road she drove. "Where is everybody?" she wondered aloud.

"Sittin' at home waiting for someone to come rescue them," replied Antwon, in between bites of a granola bar.

"Or they're afraid the roads aren't passable." JC

pulled his phone from his pocket and checked the signal, as he had every hour or two since this morning. "I wonder how widespread this thing is. The fact that no one is coming toward us is what worries me."

"Well," she argued, "if they have TV reception on the coast, they know how bad it hit us and are smart enough not to come this way."

Antwon grunted. "You keep thinkin' that, girl. Just keep believin'."

The climb into the mountains outside New Cuyama heated up the car engine, but the cold night air brought it back down again as they descended on the coastal side. By the time they reached the 101, acid burned in Niki's stomach. "Guys, shouldn't we be seeing city lights?"

As they merged onto the coastal freeway, Niki figured out why no one had been headed east. They were all going north or south, apparently hoping for safety elsewhere on the coast. Traffic moved like rush hour in downtown L.A. The freeway was a parking lot. The temperature gauge on the dashboard was nearing the peak again, and the engine made odd noises.

JC leaned over to look at the dashboard. "We're gonna kill the engine. You need to pull over."

"If anyone in front of me moves, I can." She had barely joined the traffic lane after reaching the end of the onramp.

"You've got enough room," JC said. "Crank the wheel hard."

Muttering about increasing her insurance rates, Niki felt certain she was going to hit the bumper of the SUV in front of her but she squeezed by and reached the shoulder safely. Sliding her thigh out of the way, she let JC disconnect the wiring. "Now what?"

Antwon looked out the back window at the line of headlights. "This is bigger than we thought, man. All these people are leaving town from up north."

JC held up his phone again. "Cell towers are down here, too."

Both guys looked at her as if she had the answers. "What? I left all the answers in the pocket of my other pants."

"Well, where does your sister live?" JC sat sideways, one arm braced on the dash, the other rested on the back of his seat.

"It's two or three miles from here. Does anyone have a watch?"

"Nah, I just use my phone," JC said.

"Yeah, me too," Antwon agreed.

Trying to remind herself she was capable of running a busy shift without anyone telling her how to do it, she decided she needed to act like she knew what she was doing. "I guess we have to walk to the Farmer's house."

They grabbed their water bottles and boxes of munchies and hit the pavement, walking on the shoulder of the freeway. The smell of exhaust fumes sickened Niki almost immediately. "Man, have these cars been sitting here all day? I can't breathe."

Before anyone could respond, the pavement beneath their feet rippled. Niki dropped her water and threw her arms out for balance.

JC gripped her sleeve. "Earthquake."

"No shit," said Antwon, who grabbed Niki's other arm.

Niki could see the cars bouncing, their headlight beams dancing about. People up and down the freeway began to yell. From behind them on the overpass, voices cried out and car doors slammed. A flood of people ran toward Niki and the guys, away from the bridge.

JC pushed her. "Let's get away from here."

Running on the rocking pavement was like being on a trampoline with another person. She stumbled often, but the guys jerked her upright. How they kept their balance she couldn't understand.

The shaking went on forever. Behind them, the bridge collapsed with a huge noise that sent a cloud of dust chasing the three of them. More jumped from their cars and ran. The raised section of the freeway began to buckle.

The guys ran faster, pulling Niki behind them. JC's voice carried over the noise around them. "Hurry up."

Antwon scooped up a toddler who stumbled next to her mother and carried her with him. Screams and yells rang out, then were drowned by the crunching metal and crashing cement when elevated sections of the freeway dropped to the ground beneath it.

Once the quaking stopped and people slowed, the threesome continued walking on the shoulder of the freeway. Niki's legs shook. She panted, her throat burning from breathing hard in the cold air. "Did everyone get out of their cars back there?"

"I think so," JC said. He panted hard, but wasn't winded like she was.

Antwon came back from returning the little girl to her mother. "Let's keep going. No point standing around here."

He was right. The people around them had the deer-in-headlights look. Those whose cars were on solid ground couldn't go anywhere until the cars in front of them moved. Niki's car wasn't going anywhere in its condition, and a large section of road was now missing between them and her car. She hoped the Farmers,

Crystal's family, would have suggestions for how they could get back to Bakersfield.

She glanced at the guys who walked on either side of her. What a motley crew they were. The two guys towered over her, hoofing it down the four-lane highway lit only by random headlights. The streetlamps were dark, and no lights of any kind lit up the distance. They were only a mile or so from the outskirts of the town. There should be a glow on the horizon.

The pace JC set was almost a jog, but Niki didn't complain. Walking down the freeway with no cars moving in either direction had to be the creepiest thing she could remember doing. Well, other than lying in a concrete cocoon. She knew she'd have nightmares forever from that.

From the corner of her eye, she noticed headlights crossing the field between the freeway and the town. "That's weird. I don't remember a road there."

More headlights followed the cross-country drivers. People on the freeway began to point. A squeal of feedback sounded from a semi-truck down the freeway, and a man's voice called out, "Attention, everybody! That last quake was centered in the ocean. The officials are saying we have thirty minutes to get to higher ground before a tidal wave hits."

As one, the crowd surged across the freeway, away from the coast, toward the hills and mountains. JC grabbed Niki's hand and yanked her in that direction. "Come on."

"But wait, my sister..." She plodded behind him, squeezing between the lines of parked cars. "I have to find Crystal."

"You have to live to find her. Hurry up."

They ran blindly through the weedy median

between the sections of the freeway and wove through another line of cars. Niki lost sight of Antwon in the darkness but couldn't look for him while she tried to keep up with JC. The brush tripped her repeatedly, and her shoulder hurt from JC yanking her arm.

"We're almost there," he said when she stumbled again.

The shadowed hills loomed ahead. Suddenly Niki remembered what the area looked like in the daylight. "Those are cliffs. We can't climb up there."

They had reached the dry creek bed, and the sandy soil slowed their progress. She pushed JC north toward the turnoff to Bakersfield. "Follow the creek bed. We can climb better where the hill hits the freeway. Or follow the 166 back into the mountains. That'd be easiest."

"Yeah, and most crowded. Let's hurry."

The closer they got to the freeway again, the larger the crowd grew. It made her think of the line to get in the Rise Against concert. A swarm of people wanting to be first. But this time their lives depended on it.

"How long has it been?" The slower-moving crowd allowed Niki to catch her breath.

"Maybe ten minutes. We need to move." JC rose up on his toes and looked over the mob. Once again, he yanked on her arm. "This way."

He led her to the edge of the crowd, and along with a few young men, they ran through the shoulder or up into the weeds, skirting the hillside.

Niki fought to keep up, but JC was unrelenting. At one point her took her by the waist and lifted her down from the pavement and jumped after her. He pushed her ahead, nearly running her over.

"We have to get up the hill."

"We're like ten miles from the ocean," she spat out

between gasps for air. "How far can the water come?"

"It depends on how strong the quake was. In Japan it came in at least six miles in some places, maybe ten in others. But there are no buildings or anything between us and the shore to slow it down."

"Okay, okay, I'm going." She skirted some sagebrush and tried to hurry while walking across the side of a hill. She sucked in air as hard as she could. "This would be a lot easier if we were on the road."

"They aren't moving fast enough over there."

She had to wonder why it was so important to him that she get to safety, why he didn't just leave her behind. He didn't know her, other than the occasional sighting across the apartment complex. He was one of the ones who'd teased her in school. He still called her Mouse. But for some reason she couldn't tell him to quit worrying about her.

It was nice to have someone do that for a change.

The crowd began to thin as they reached midway up the rise. People either felt they'd gotten high enough, or they were too tired to go on. But JC urged her forward. Finally, he guided her up the bank on the side of the road and helped her clear the fence at the top.

The moon had come out from behind the clouds, but it was only half full, not offering much light. Niki could make out the sea of people filling the hillside, and the line of motionless cars and trucks on the 101. Somewhere beyond the black stretch of farmland lay the ocean. If the officials were right, the ocean was going to be a lot closer any minute.

Her nerves were too jagged to wait calmly. "Do you think there'll really be a tidal wave?"

"I don't know. But we're high enough to be safe."

As far as she could see on the hills to the south, people were milling about. She thought about asking if anyone was from Santa Maria. If they knew her sister. She prayed Crystal heard the warning and had evacuated with her parents. "How am I going to find her?"

"What?" JC asked from beside her. He had his hands in the pockets of his hoodie, his shoulders slouched as he stared into the dark night.

"Just thinking out loud about Crystal."

"We'll find her."

His words angered her. It was crazy, but they did. She bit her tongue to keep from lashing out. She didn't want platitudes, and there was no way he could think she would locate her sister before the world was back to normal.

Whenever that would be.

Chapter Five

A murmur rippled through the mass of people on the hillside, alerting Niki something was up. JC nudged her arm with his elbow. "Here it comes."

The people around them made too much noise to hear the sound of water breaking against the land. Only when the white froth at the front of the wave reached the light of the cars on the freeway could Niki finally see the water.

"I thought it would be bigger. Like in the movies. When it swamps a ship."

"Those are rogue waves. Watch, it's still coming."

The ocean pushed against the lines of cars, sweeping the southbound lanes clean as it swamped the freeway. It surged forward and pushed the northbound cars over the side, piling them up against the foot of the hills.

As far as Niki could see, water covered the land. It was so calm, so quiet as it rolled inward, the level rising when it met the hills. Not at all violent like the earthquake. A stealthy, surreal monster slipping up on the unaware.

"What about Santa Maria? All the cities along the

coast?"

JC shook his head. "Buildings would slow the water down. Some of them might withstand the pressure, but others might get knocked down. That's why they said to get out."

Her knees turned into oatmeal. *Crystal.* Did Crystal make it out okay? *A tight band pressed against her chest and she couldn't draw in a breath. She gasped, flinging her arms about. She felt like she was caught in a wave, being held under long past when the air in her lungs ran out. Her lungs burned. A dark shadow swallowed her.*

"Nicole!" JC's voice called from a great distance. She reached out, unable to find him.

Unable to draw a breath to cry out, Niki prayed for help.

A pale mist formed in front of Niki. Anne's face smiled at her. She mouthed something but Niki couldn't hear.

With another desperate gasp, Niki's lungs finally filled with air. "What? I can't hear you."

The shadow around Niki cleared, and she found herself sitting in the grass, with JC holding her upper arms. The people around her had cleared a space as if her fit of panic were contagious.

JC looked down at her. "I asked if you were okay."

Anne's face vanished. Apparently JC couldn't see her. Niki wasn't about to tell anyone she was seeing her dead friend. "Oh…okay. Yeah, I'm fine."

Antwon pushed his way through the crowd and JC stood. "You found us."

"Yeah."

Niki smiled in honest relief when she saw him. "Where'd you go?"

"I carried those kids up the hill for that lady. She

had two little ones and a baby. There was no way they'd be able to run fast enough."

"That's cool." Niki wasn't able to put how she really felt into words. *Ohmygod, no way. You really risked yourself to save some stranger's kids?* She wanted to believe she would have done the same, but she'd seen the family getting out of their car and it never occurred to her to help then, much less when the tidal wave warning came. "That's really cool, Antwon."

She was beginning to revise her opinion of how she reacted in an emergency. These two guys were the kind you wanted around when things got crazy. Herself? Not so much.

Antwon turned back to JC. "What happened to her? I heard her crying out."

"Panic attack, I guess."

Niki pushed to her feet between them. "Hello. I'm right here. I can hear you talking about me."

Shoving her hair out of her face, she peered up at Antwon, but it was too dark to make out his expression. "I don't get panic attacks. I was upset about everything that's happened today. Or yesterday. Whatever. But I'm fine now."

There was no way she could explain the feeling that had come over her just moments before. She was in the tidal wave. Water rose quickly around her, and she floated upward with it. Then her head hit the ceiling. But the water kept rising. She fought against it, tried to swim to a door or window but was disoriented.

When Anne's face had appeared, a sense of peace crept in to the tiny spaces in her body where panic lived. Niki could swear she'd been drowning, but she stood on top of the hill well above the water. It didn't make sense. And the only reason she could find to explain what she'd felt was if she'd been experiencing what her sister was.

No. It's not true.

Crystal had to be all right, or there was no reason for Niki to keep trying to get through it all. All the adrenaline from the quakes and tidal wave faded, and she suddenly felt like she'd been run over by an entire football team. She tried not to lean on JC, but it was hard to remain standing on spaghetti legs. "What do we do now?"

The guys shrugged. Antwon spoke first. "You didn't find your sister."

"I know. But I'm cold, and I'm hungry." *And I think I'm going to cry.* She hated that she always wanted to cry when the worst was over. "I can't think clearly."

JC looked up the hill where most of the people mingled. "There's only a few cars that didn't get washed away. They'll never get all these people to the valley, or wherever they want to go."

"Maybe when the water goes down, they can go home." Antwon pulled up the zipper on his jacket when an ocean breeze kicked up.

"If they still have homes to go to. But what about the ones who were on the road? If they had houses, would they have left home? They would have camped out in their yards." JC looked from Antwon to Niki. "There are a lot of people who need food and shelter now. I wonder if FEMA has enough resources for something this big."

Antwon looked around. "Maybe we can get some sleep. When the sun comes up, we can sort things out then."

Allowing the guys to lead her down the hill where the breeze was less noticeable, Niki shivered. Lisa's coat was thick, but it couldn't keep out the chill that invaded her very bones. She would never feel warm again. Never feel safe.

They sat on the cold, dead grass. The ground suddenly shook. Children cried out. A woman screamed like the earth had opened up in front of her. The shaking was brief, a small aftershock, but Niki's body trembled long after the hillside stilled.

She shivered again and leaned closer to JC for warmth. Some of the families had blankets and water. One woman bottle-fed an infant. Yet Niki sat with two guys she barely knew, wearing a borrowed coat, with no socks or underwear under her uniform. The comparison made her giggle.

JC turned. "What?"

"Nothing." She laughed again, the bubbles slipping out against her will.

"What's so funny?"

Drawing her knees up to her chest, she hugged herself. "It's not funny. But I can't stop laughing."

Antwon grunted. "So tell us anyway. I could use a laugh."

"It's really stupid." Her nose began to run and she sniffled. "Look at these people. They were prepared for an emergency. They have blankets and food. And water. I'm thirsty. I dropped my bottle on the freeway."

JC pulled his water bottle from his hoodie pocket, while Antwon's appeared from up his sleeve. They both held the bottles out to her.

She hesitated before taking JC's and downing a quick swallow. Handing it back, she said, "Thanks. You wouldn't happen to have a granola bar in there, too, would you?"

He didn't, but Antwon did. When she took it from him, she tore it open and broke it in three pieces, giving the guys each one. The oats and raisins tasted heavenly, better than chocolate fudge brownie ice cream. Almost.

Even taking tiny bites, it was gone too soon. She sighed. No sense wishing for a pillow or blanket. Hoodie pockets weren't that deep.

"Better?" JC asked.

"I guess so. I'm really tired. I'm getting loopy. It bugs me that everyone else in the world is so prepared, and I'm not. The only thing I was prepared for was being called in to work when I'm not on the schedule."

"That's not a bad thing," Antwon said softly. "I bet your boss appreciates that."

"But look at me." As if they could see her on a dark hillside in the middle of the night. "Even if I was prepared, it's all lost with my car now. On its way out to sea, where it'll rust away and become a mansion for tiny fish."

The bouts of hysteric laughter were shifting into even more hysterical tears. "All I have is my stupid uniform. It's the end of the world, and we're all about to die but we don't know it yet."

Her voice rose in pitch and she tried to keep her volume low, but she couldn't stop the warbling, pity-me words from pouring out. "I don't want to die in my freakin' Taco Shack uniform."

A tear rolled down her cheek and she batted it away with the back of her hand. She rested her forehead on her knees and wished she were anywhere but on a hillside in the middle of nowhere. She wished she was home, warm and in bed. Asleep. Blissfully unaware of what was happening in the world.

She felt a heavy weight across her shoulders as JC's arm came to rest there. He sat awkwardly beside her as if not certain how to offer comfort. "You're not going to die."

"You're sure?" Her words echoed in the hollow between her legs and chest. "Because it'd really suck if I had to spend the afterlife serving tacos."

Antwon snickered. "That'd be funny, if we went to heaven in what we were wearing when we died. Think of all the people who die having sex."

JC's arm shook, but he didn't make a sound. "That's dumb, man. Funny, but dumb."

The warmth of his arm seeped through her coat with an oddly comforting sensation. It calmed her. She began to feel sleepy, but couldn't give in to it. Not with so many people around. She was so tempted to lean into JC's shoulder, pillow her head there and rest. Give in for once and let someone else keep watch that everything was going to be okay.

But it wasn't, and she couldn't relax until she found her sister.

JC pointed up at the sky. "Look at that."

All she saw was stars. Lots and lots of stars, since there were no lights to dilute them. "What?"

"That asteroid, or whatever."

Antwon leaned back on his arms and stretched out his long legs. "It's moving too slowly. Probably a satellite."

Niki decided it was a guy thing. "No big deal, whatever it is."

"What if an asteroid started all this? If it hit up north, it could have caused the big quake." JC continued to watch the sky.

She rolled her eyes. "What are the chances of that? Doesn't NASA have ways of monitoring asteroids? They would send up a ship to break it up. They've made enough movies about it."

Antwon snorted. "You believe what you see in the

movies?"

She was grateful the guys couldn't see the flush creeping up her neck. "No. Of course not. But they would at least have given us some warning so we could evacuate."

JC had the nerve to muss her hair. "I like your world, Mouse."

"I told you not to call me that." The nickname hit her like a punch in the stomach. Why, freakin' why, did she bring them along? She should have gone home with Lisa, where she'd have blankets and a tent, at least. Lisa camped a lot on her one weekend off each month. They even had a pop-up trailer. They were probably living in it now.

Lisa used to tell her everything happened for a reason. For the life of her, Niki couldn't find any reason to be stranded with these two guys. A few years ago she wouldn't have been surprised by it, but she thought she'd outgrown her stupid decisions.

Apparently not. And this time, it looked like the decision could be her last, if they didn't find food and shelter.

~*~

JC tried to look down at Niki's head where it rested on his shoulder, but he couldn't see her face. Her body had gone limp, like she was asleep. He gently rolled her to her side and let her rest on the ground. He motioned to Antwon as he stood.

"What's up?" Antwon stretched and rolled to his feet.

"I want to look at our options."

"Options for what?"

"Food. Transportation. There's no way we're walking

back to Taft without food and water. There are some reservoirs and ponds between here and there, but I don't want to waste time searching for them. We could end up lost."

"Wish our phones worked. We could Google Map the area."

A motor roared to life on the highway. JC broke into a run. "Hurry!"

As they stumbled down the hill, JC saw a pickup truck loaded with people. "Wait up," he called. The driver revved the engine again as JC and Antwon hopped onto the rear bumper.

"Let's go," someone shouted.

JC grabbed the tailgate to keep from being thrown off. He threw a leg into the bed, which was too crowded to climb into. Antwon straddled the tailgate, too. A couple of guys grabbed for their sleeves and belt loops to keep them from falling out.

"Hang on," one yelled. "He'll slow down when he reaches the top of the hill."

The wind bit into JC's face. He wanted to grab his beanie to be sure it stayed on but was afraid he'd get tossed out. He wasn't sure how fast they were going but landing on asphalt at that speed would hurt.

The driver kept an easy speed, but it didn't make the ride any warmer. JC almost wished they'd go faster to get to the city sooner. Not that he was looking forward to what he had to do. But it had to be done, if they were going to survive.

JC guessed the time to be around one or two in the morning when they reached Taft. The pickup truck pulled over on the side of the road and most of the men in the back hopped out, calling their thanks.

"Yeah, thanks, man," JC said.

Antwon tugged at his hoodie as if it had been nearly blown off, pulling down the sleeves and adjusting it on his shoulders. "Where to, now?"

"My dad's house."

The one thing JC had always liked about Antwon was he didn't ask a lot of questions. He fell into step beside JC and walked quietly. Kaylee would have been hounding him. *Where are we going? Why? What are you gonna do?*

Her laugher filled his head. He drew in a breath and huffed it out. Surviving was going to be tough. Hopefully people were right, and the pain of losing someone would go away. To shut it out, he started making a mental list of what to look for at his dad's house.

He purposely avoided thinking about what he'd say if his dad was there. He had too many years' worth of stuff he planned to say. But there was no point now.

They turned down the street his dad lived on. With only the weak moonlight to see by, he could tell the houses were badly damaged. A dog barked in the distance, and a man's voice told it to shut up. The fences had better be standing after the quake, considering the kind of dogs the neighbors owned. He wouldn't want to meet up with one.

He motioned toward his dad's driveway and silently led the way around the side of the small house. The walls were upright, but glass crunched under his feet when he walked past a window. He reached over the fence and unlatched the gate.

Antwon followed, whispering, "Are you sure this is your dad's house, man?"

"Yeah."

"I thought you didn't have a dad."

"Everyone's got a dad, dude, whether they want one

or not."

Crossing the yard, JC went to the detached garage and felt for the lock. It was latched tightly. He wondered what the odds were the key was in the same place after ten years. He felt along the ground for the plaster turtle. Finding it right where he expected, he twisted off the left hind foot and felt around in the small cavity. His finger hit the key.

Grinning he pulled it out and went back to the padlock. "We're good to go."

"Man, I don't like this. Isn't this breakin' and enterin'? 'Cause I just know we're gonna get caught and you know who they're gonna nail it on? The black guy. They always blame it on the black guy. And which one of us is the black guy? Oh, yeah. Me."

JC glared but realized it had no effect in the dark. He'd known Antwon for years and the guy thought he was Chris Rock. "Will you stop talking like a punk-ass kid?"

"I *am* a punk-ass kid."

"I'm beginning to believe you. But talk the way you normally do. You sound like a straight-to-video movie." JC lifted the door and peered into the black space.

"That's what my aunt tells me, too. But I still don't like what we're doing. What, exactly, are we doing?"

"My dad has a couple of dirt bikes, or he used to. And he gave me a crossbow one year, but he kept it at his place. We could really use all of that. I wish we had some light." As he worked his way into the garage, he saw everything had fallen from the shelves, and stacks of plastic totes had tumbled, some losing their lids, others splitting when they fell.

He ignored the big red tool box, even though he knew all those tools would be nice to have on hand.

Their immediate need was for transportation. Any hunting equipment he could find would be a bonus.

The sky was beginning to brighten when JC decided it was time to go. They'd scored the two dirt bikes, the crossbow and two arrows in its case, a folding knife, and a battery operated lantern, and a few other odds and ends he thought might come in handy. A 5-gallon gas can held enough fuel to top off the bikes, and he prayed they'd been used recently enough that they ran. He loaded the stuff into a milk crate that he strapped on the rear fender of one bike with a couple of rubber cords. With one last glance around in the growing light, he noticed the day pack that once held a tent. He grabbed it and swung it on his back, then lowered the garage door and locked it again.

"Won't your dad be pissed when he sees his stuff gone?"

"I don't even know for sure if he's dead or alive. One of these bikes was mine, and the crossbow. The other stuff…well, we'll call it back child support." He rolled the bike down the driveway, with Antwon following him. As much as he felt he had a right to take what he had, he really didn't want to see the old man today. Or any other day.

When they got a few houses away, he straddled the bike. He glanced at Antwon. "Cross your fingers." Kicking the starter, he grinned when it grunted and quit. It purred to life on the second try. Antwon took a bit longer to get his going, but as soon as he did, JC drove off.

Chapter Six

Niki woke to the sound of a baby crying, only the sound wasn't filtered through her apartment walls. She felt the damp grass beneath her cheek and jolted upright as the prior day rushed back into her memory.

She was alone in a sea of refugees on the hillside east of Santa Maria. JC and Antwon were nowhere to be seen, although a water bottle was propped in the dirt beside her. She took a quick drink and stuck the bottle in her coat pocket. There was no way she was going to lose this little bit of water, not knowing how long it had to last. Standing, she searched the area for the guys. Her back complained when she climbed up the hillside. She'd only gotten a couple hours sleep, yet her muscles felt like she'd slept a week on a rock.

From the top of the hill, she surveyed the 101 Freeway below. Most of the water had receded, leaving the cars and some rubble tossed about like toys in a child's playroom. The structure of the freeway didn't appear any more damaged than what the quake had done, but the cars were probably not capable of being driven after being in the water. Sand covered the area where weeds had been.

Around her, everyone seemed to be waiting for help to arrive. Since most of the cities on the coast had probably been hit by the tsunami, and the central valley had been destroyed by the earthquake, she wondered where they thought help would come from. If they were lucky, emergency crews from cities farther north and south, or east of the Sierra Nevada Mountains were responding to the coast.

JC and Antwon had vanished during the night. So much for helping her find Crystal. Their leaving was probably for the better, since it would be easier to scavenge food for one than for three. She kept telling herself this when her stomach growled, and again when the single swallow of water she allowed herself didn't stem the hunger.

Niki couldn't just sit and wait for help to arrive. One by one, she went to the small groupings of refugees and asked if they knew the Farmers. The people who'd been on the freeway came from farther north, leaving her to wonder if anyone from Santa Maria had escaped in time.

As she worked her way back toward the eastbound highway, her hopes dwindled. Hopes of finding Crystal, hopes of getting back to Bakersfield. How long would it take to walk more than a hundred miles?

Without food and water, the journey would be impossible. Even the closest town of any size was too far to walk to without supplies. She was stuck like everyone else, needing help to have any chance of survival.

She hated having to rely on other people. Even more than she hated working on her birthday.

Standing on the slope of the highway above the high tide mark, she felt betrayed. She'd thought JC was going to stick around, help her out. They would have helped each other out. Turns out he was a loser, like she'd always suspected. And no matter how tempting it might be to have a friend at her side, no matter how much his presence meant she wasn't alone, it was better he left now than somewhere down the road when she really needed him.

At the base of the hill, where the cars lay scattered about, she saw an occasional fish flopping in the last throes of death. Sea gulls swarmed and were feasting and fighting over the bodies. Her stomach growled. No way was she going to fight a bunch of birds for a sushi breakfast. She wasn't that hungry. Yet.

The high-pitched whine of a small motorcycle engine grew in the distance behind her. Niki turned around and watched the empty highway. A pair of dirt bikes came over a small rise, one white rider, one black. They came down the westbound lanes, reached a dirt through-way in the median and crossed over to where she stood.

She shook her head as they approached. An evil thought about where they might have stolen the bikes passed through her head and she bit her lip. Even during PMS she wasn't normally this bitchy. JC brought out the worst in her. Or the earthquake did. She couldn't quite convince herself it was only the disasters that had her on edge.

He smiled slightly when he pulled to a stop in front of her. It was the first smile she'd seen on his face since he dug her out of the apartment rubble. Antwon rolled up beside him, his ever-present cocky grin splitting his face, his billowy hair fluffed out in a huge 'fro. On the back of one of the bikes was a milk crate filled with supplies.

"What did you guys do? Rob someone?"

"Not really," JC answered. "The bikes were my dad's. He lives in Taft. I couldn't find him to ask if I could borrow them. I figure he owed my mom, only she isn't here to collect."

Antwon pulled a pair of gloves from his hoodie and gave them to Niki. "We thought your hands might get cold on the ride."

"Thanks." They were butt-ugly gray, fake leather gardening gloves, but she knew she would appreciate them in the days to come. "How did you guys get all the way to Taft and back? And why the hell didn't you tell me you were leaving?"

All her fears swelled up at once and she couldn't keep back the tears. She drew in a shaky breath. "I thought you guys had left me."

Antwon looked away. JC lost his smile, his brows drawing together in a frown. "You were sleeping. Some guys were able to get their truck running and offered to give people a ride. A ton of guys jumped in the bed of the truck. We had to hang onto the tailgate all the way to New Cuyama. There wasn't time to get you."

He looked more hurt than angry. And he did come back for her. She chewed her lip for a moment before apologizing. "Sorry. I didn't mean to bitch. I guess I'm wound up a little tight."

JC took out a zippered baggie of jerky. "Have something to eat and we can decide what do to next."

Grabbing the package a bit more roughly than was polite, she muttered her thanks and walked to the side of the road to sit. After chewing, and chewing, the first mouthful, she looked down at the bag. "What kind of jerky is this?"

"Venison, I think."

She held out the meat in her hand, debating spitting out what was in her mouth, but it didn't taste awful. Not really good, but still… "You gave me deer meat?" Swallowing was hard.

"It's all I could find." He stared down at his shoes, making her feel like shit again.

"I'm glad you found it. But warn me next time. Okay?"

JC grunted, but the sound was almost lost under the growl her stomach gave. Niki tugged off another piece of jerky with her teeth and started chewing. Realizing she still held the bag, she offered it to the guys. As they each took a piece, she asked, "Did you see any emergency crews?"

Antwon leaned forward to see around JC, who sat between them. "Some local workers were cutting away trees in the road and moving power lines in case they went live again. Didn't see anyone from the power companies."

"Nothing that looked like FEMA or the local Red Cross or anything, either." JC scratched his head through his beanie. "I thought emergency crews went through drills for this stuff, so they'd know what to do when it happened. Where is everyone?"

"It's like they're too busy saving themselves to rescue anyone else," Antwon agreed.

JC met her gaze. "I saw a bunch of bodies lined up under sheets at the football field."

Niki swallowed the half-chewed jerky in her mouth. "They're not burying them there, are they? That sucks."

He shook his head. "Probably just need a big enough place to keep the bodies until they're identified. Hope it stays cold. There were a lot of bodies there, but a lot of the houses were flattened. At least in the older section of town where my dad lives."

Shivering, Niki wrapped her arms around herself. "I need to let Crystal know I'm not dead." She couldn't quit thinking about that.

"We're gonna do that, Niki. We'll find a way."

She climbed to her feet. "We should get going. Will your bike carry two?"

JC stretched like a cat as he stood. He'd probably been up all night and looked exhausted. "Yeah, you're skinny. I think we have enough gas to get us back to Taft, at least. There's something you should know, though."

"What?"

"We were warned about coming back here. We're only half an hour or so from the nuclear plant up the coast. We should get back over the hill right away. There could be radiation leaking in the air."

Her heart stopped. "We can't go look for Crystal?"

"She's not there. You know her family would've bugged out. And they'll have the city blocked off to keep looters out. Her parents'll keep her safe and we can watch for them to come through Taft."

"What, are we going to sit in the middle of the road and check IDs as people come to town?"

He shook his head. "They're setting up stations where people are checking in, making lists of who's alive and who's dead. So we'll check the lists until we find her."

No one on the hills around them showed any signs of concern about the nuclear plant. Niki didn't know if the plant was even online, or if there was a danger when one was offline. She knew from Japan's recent problems that earthquakes, tidal waves and nuclear plants didn't mix. She needed to make smart decisions to stay alive long enough to find her sister.

"Okay. Let's get out of here. Are you guys okay to drive?"

Antwon grinned and nodded, his hair bobbing. "We had a couple of energy drinks. We'll be awake all day."

As Antwon straddled his dirt bike, she looked at the milk crate behind him. "Where are your helmets? We can't ride without helmets."

Laughing, Antwon kicked his engine to life. "I don't think the highway patrol is handing out too many tickets, Mouse."

She gritted her teeth. "Don't call me that. My name is Niki."

JC sat waiting on his bike. "Come on. We need to get out of here."

Niki climbed on behind him and tried to figure out what to do with her feet as he accelerated up the hill. She nearly fell off the back of the bike. Grabbing at JC's hoodie, she wrapped her arms around his waist, her thighs pressing against his. Butterflies fluttered in her stomach. She hadn't been this close to a guy in a long time.

The wind picked up as they gained speed and she added to that thought. *Too bad we have nowhere to shower.*

The guys slowed down to city speeds when they reached the outskirts of Taft, but they kept going on the highway through town. Niki yelled into JC's ear. "Why didn't we stop?"

"They're setting up a tent city at Lake Buena Vista. We might be able to score some blankets and sleeping bags when we get there."

The image that provoked left her with mixed emotions. Yay, she could lie down and get warm, but boo, they were sharing a tent? The campgrounds at the lake had showers and bathrooms, though, a major plus. She hadn't been able to go behind a bush with hundreds of refugees sitting around on that hill.

JC tipped his head and called out, "We can fish in the lake, too."

Niki wondered what they'd catch them with, and was still wondering an hour later when the guys waded in the water trying to catch fish in their hands. They looked like little kids, swooping and splashing. They looked like they were having fun. JC finally pulled out a pocketknife and cut a switch from a small tree and they took turns stabbing into the water.

As she watched, she combed her fingers through the mat her hair had become, with dust from her apartment building cemented in it. Picking at some clumps in the ends, she couldn't tell her highlights from the mousy brown strands.

The guys seemed quite pleased with themselves when they brought her two average-size trout. She eyed the fish warily. She was not eating something with eyes attached, especially after seeing the sea gulls pecking at the dead fish on the coast. "I hope someone has a lighter, and you plan to clean those things."

"No problem," JC said. He wandered off toward the brush where some family groups had set up camp. When he returned, he had a bundle of sticks in one hand and a burning branch in another. He dropped the wood in front of her and she quickly laid them into a circle.

He knelt and laid the branch onto the dried grass Antwon added to the pile. "We need to find enough wood to keep this burning, so we don't have to keep begging for a light."

Niki watched, kind of amazed, as JC stuck a green branch into the fish and propped it with rocks to lie above the fire. "Boy Scout?"

"Nah. Dad used to take me here when I was a kid. Before he left, I mean."

She nodded. The area they were from, Oildale, had a good number of broken families. Like her own, in a manner of speaking. But that was a break of a different kind. She shut the door on that thought and looked at Antwon. "Where's your family? Aren't they worried about you? Did you lose your house, too?"

"Yeah, gas line broke next door to my uncle's house. The whole block had to evacuate. My uncle was already gone to work. My auntie was gonna take her six kids to her mama's house. I said I'd crash with friends until they let us go back. I figured she didn't need one more mouth to worry about."

He didn't mention parents, but she didn't push. She didn't talk about hers, either. "Where do you work? Or should I say, did you work?"

"Out here in the oilfields. I'm a welder's assistant."

JC snorted. "He means a grunt. Laborer."

Antwon looked unperturbed. "Whatever. Pays good, when it's not raining."

Just then, a huge crash rang out down the lake and people began screaming and yelling. Niki and the guys jumped up and ran toward the noise. In the parking lot, a crowd of people gathered around a pickup truck and large camp trailer. Drawing near, Niki noticed a child's legs sticking out from beneath the side of the trailer. A wheel had fallen off, and somehow the child was trapped underneath when it lurched.

Men gathered around the trailer and were trying to lift. Someone tried to force a jack under the edge of the trailer, but they couldn't raise it high enough to use the jack. Antwon and JC shoved their way in and squatted down, grabbing the trailer frame on either side of the wheel. Antwon's body began to shake. His legs trembled, causing his pant legs to shiver. He straightened slowly, the trailer rising with him. Someone yelled, and several people crawled underneath to pull the little girl free.

They carried her away and a man gave the all clear. The trailer dropped with a *clang*. Antwon turned around, his face dark, his features drained. JC watched him with an odd expression. Niki joined them and they walked back to their campsite. JC adjusted the fish over the flames, and they sat around the fire.

Antwon kept his head down. Niki spoke softly. "Are you okay?"

"Yeah, I'm fine."

"That was really incredible, dude, how did you do that?" JC leaned one arm over his bent leg, the other leg curled on the ground. "I mean, no one is that strong."

"I don't know, man. I don't know what happened. I started to shake and the thing just lifted off the ground."

"I know. I felt it," JC said.

"What are you talking about?" Niki asked.

"Back there," JC explained, nodding in the direction of the trailer. "That wasn't all of us lifting. It was him."

Antwon peered up at him. "That's crazy, man. There's no way I could lift it all myself."

"JC," Niki argued, "I was watching. You all lifted."

"We all had our hands on it but I know how hard I was working and I didn't even need to be there. Antwon did it all by himself."

"No way," Antwon disagreed.

"I won't argue with you, dude. I've heard of people getting amazing strength in an emergency. I'll just say I hope you can do it again if we ever need it." JC lifted the branch with the fish and poked at them. "I think these are about done. Mouse, if you find a rock or something to put it on, I'll cut some meat off here for you."

The subject wasn't closed, but Niki let it drop for now.

Chapter Seven

Darkness fell and the stars were as plentiful as the night before. The air was still, except for soft voices from around the lake. Refugees continued to arrive all evening, apparently hearing about the availability of water, fish and toilets. She wondered where they all came from and how long they'd all be there. In the morning, she'd ask if anyone knew the Farmers.

After wandering away for a bit, JC returned to the fire and sat close to her. "Your coat isn't warm enough for a night out here. I wish we had some blankets."

They'd been unable to find any sleeping bags, but had set up the tent using some tree branches in place of missing poles. Niki studied JC as they sat in front of the tent. She wondered how long it would take before she got used to having him worry about her. It made her stomach feel strange. Good strange. She smiled, just a little. "I'll be okay."

On the other side of the fire, Antwon sharpened a stick against a rock. He hadn't said much since they ate. Since they'd helped rescue the girl. Niki wondered what he was thinking, but didn't know him well enough to ask. Not that she knew JC any better, but there was something different between them since he'd pulled her from her apartment.

She turned to JC, who was playing with the drawstring on his hood. "What do you think L.A. looks like? I haven't even seen any planes bringing in supplies. Any jets, period."

He caught her gaze and studied her a bit before answering. "It's hard to say. Word around here is worse than what I was hearing this morning. This is big, Mouse. The Big One. People are talking about volcanoes and quakes, tsunamis and tidal waves. And not only in North America. All over the world. CB and ham radios are still working and people are reaching out."

She drew in a breath against the knot in her gut. "God, I hope Crystal is okay. She's all the family I've got."

"I know. I heard about your folks when we were in high school."

"Oh great." Niki combed her fingers through her hair. "I'll bet everyone loved that. The headlines were bad enough. 'Oildale Couple Arrested for Manufacturing.' As if they were the only people in town cooking methamphetamine."

"Actually, you got as much sympathy at school as there were smartasses making jokes about it."

"Why did they even talk about it? My parents' trial was over by the end of my freshman year. I was old news by the time I transferred to North High, senior year."

"News never gets old in high school, Mouse."

There was that nickname again, the one she hated. "Why did they call me that? Why do you still call me that? My friends call me Niki. I wish you'd use that name."

He pulled off his cap and set it down beside him, scratching his head. His hair was a lot longer than she expected, and curly. The ends glinted golden in the firelight, as if he spent a lot of time in the sun. "I think Mitchell started it. Said you looked like a mouse the way you scurried through the halls, sticking close to the walls."

"How else was I supposed to get through? Look at me. I'm 5'4", not tall enough to even see through the crowds, much less push my way between those steroid-popping football linemen."

With a shrug, JC said, "I thought it was kind of cute. Like you."

She blinked and mentally repeated that. No one had ever acted as if she was cute, except her freakish friends. Okay, so she had dyed the tips of her hair black and pink at the beginning of the last school year, and tended to wear Goth makeup and chunky-soled boots with her jeans long after they were out of style. Her nails were painted black more often than not. But in truth, except for the nickname she earned in the hallways, she figured no one noticed her.

And she'd left all that angst behind. Kept her nails cut short, only wore a little makeup. Lisa said she'd go farther at work if she didn't look like a drama queen.

The ground shook hard enough she couldn't ignore it, but not enough to make her panic. Throughout the day, small tremblers struck, so she was getting used to the little rumbles. This one was closer to a small quake than an aftershock.

The guys didn't even react, so she willed her heart to settle down. Her mind left the horrors of high school, drifted past their immediate problems to the bigger picture. In all the emergency preparedness manuals at the Taco Shack, they'd never mentioned worldwide disasters. "What's going to happen to us? To the world, everybody? I mean, when disaster hits anywhere America rolls in to help. But what if we're the lucky ones and everywhere else has been hit worse? What if there is no one to save us?"

Antwon's hands stilled. "I don't know. Who rides to the rescue if the Avengers all get killed?"

"This isn't a comic book, Antwon."

He poked his sharpened stick into the dirt and tossed down the rock. "I know. I was makin' a point. And they're graphic novels, not comic books."

JC coughed. "I didn't want to say anything, but what if this is only the beginning? Is the world dying, or just shedding its skin?"

His voice calmed her at the same time his words stirred up panic. Looking up through her bangs, she studied JC. She hadn't paid a lot of attention to his looks, but his face had filled out since graduation, softening the angles and making him more like the actors her friends drooled over. Yeah, he looked good, if she thought about it. He was always just another guy she had seen around school but hadn't really known. Too bad it took an earthquake to make her notice. He seemed like someone she would want as a friend, and they'd finally gotten together only to watch the world die.

In the firelight, he had more color to his skin, the line between his brows was gone. Was he thinking about his family? "I'm sorry about your mom and sister," she said.

His Adam's apple bobbed as he swallowed. "Yeah. It sucks. But what can we do?"

"I saw your sister sometimes playing with other

kids at the apartments. She seemed so happy."

"She was always happy. We had different dads. I think that made a difference."

Niki could understand that. "Yours was a lousy dad, too, huh?"

Grimacing, he reached out and stirred the fire. "Lousy is a good word for it. He yelled a lot. By the time he finally walked out on us, I thought JC stood for Jesus Christ. I was six."

She shifted her legs, which unintentionally brought her closer to him. She didn't pull away. "That sucks. At least my parents pretended to love us."

"I got over it. Are you cold?" He opened his jacket and pulled one side across her back.

"A little. Wish we had blankets." The weight of his arm felt reassuring and she wanted to lean against his shoulder. She was tired of being strong. She let her head drop against him.

"We'll go back to Taft tomorrow and see if we can find some blankets. And look for your sister. As long as we keep the fire going tonight, we'll stay warm." He spoke against her head, where he rested his cheek.

Some of the tension drained from her muscles. As she relaxed, she stared past the fire into the dark lake. She had been adrift ever since her parents were first arrested. Sent to live in foster homes, she and her sister clung together. But Crystal had been younger, all of five when it started, nine when their trial ended. Crystal blossomed with the attention and love they received from the Farmers, the couple who took them in. And Niki had rebelled against it.

She had fought with her foster parents because she didn't know how to accept love and kindness. Lisa had helped her see that. Her parents had been self-absorbed, so having new emotions surround her in the new home was more than she could bear. Add in her awakening hormones and she hadn't been a fun person to be around. She'd bounced from home to home, then group home to group home. By the time she aged out of the foster system last April, she had the job at Taco Shack working under Lisa, and began to settle down.

Moonlight glimmered on the lake, catching her eye. The water rippled, as if something had dropped in, and light rose from the center of the circle. The light took on human form and as it did, the form became Anne's.

Niki gasped and sat up straight. Anne hovered over the water reaching an arm out, her lips moving.

"What is it?" JC asked. He and Antwon looked around into the dark night.

"It's Anne."

"Your friend?"

Niki nodded. "She keeps talking to me but I can't hear her."

"She's gone, Mouse. Sorry. Niki. Anne's gone now."

"I know she's dead, but she's right there." She pointed toward the moon's reflection. "Can't you see her? Why can't you see her? How come only I can see her?"

Antwon spoke in a gentle voice. "She was your friend. Maybe she wants you to know she's okay."

Anne smiled and vanished. Niki nervously combed fingers through her hair and wove it into a loose braid. "I've known other people who died and I never saw them. I don't get it."

"I don't get a lot of things," Antwon said. "Like what happened at the trailer."

JC rolled to his feet. "Gotta take a walk. I'll be right back."

Niki watched him walk away, then turned back to

Antwon. "You mean how you lifted the trailer? So you did do it."

He nodded. "As soon as I touched the frame, my body started to jerk like I touched an electrical socket. I mean, I felt electricity run through me and couldn't let go if I wanted to. And then the trailer, it sort of lifted all by itself."

"Maybe it was the urgency of it all, adrenaline. You know. People lift cars off victims all the time."

"Yeah, I guess." He didn't look convinced as he went back to sharpening sticks.

JC came back into the ring of light, his arms holding blankets. "Look what I got us." He passed one to Antwon and one to Niki. "They only had two extras."

Extras. Niki repeated the word in her head and hated herself for thinking he might have, well, *acquired* them when no one was looking. She took the one he offered her. "Thank you. But, what about you? Here, you keep it."

He shook his head as he sat next to her. "I'll be okay. My hoodie is warm enough."

"That's crazy. What about your legs? Here, we can share it." She shook it out, carefully avoiding the fire, and draped one side over JC's legs. Curling up in her half, she sighed. "That feels good. I was so cold."

JC smiled. It faded quickly, but the sadness didn't return to his face. Once again her thoughts went toward the future. Beyond finding Crystal. Beyond food and shelter. How would they all live? Would they even survive whatever was to come?

All the worrying, the fear and exercise of her day, built to an overwhelming point and she needed to lie down. Her exhaustion was probably the only thing keeping her from totally panicking, or finding a hole to hide in. She stretched her legs and leaned back on one elbow. "I need to rest," she told JC.

"Oh, right." He handed her his half of the blanket. "Go get some sleep."

She rose, watching to see if anyone else was coming. Only after she lay down on the plastic floor of the tent did the guys come in and zip the door shut.

JC lay down beside her, underneath the blanket, but he seemed to be keeping as much distance between them as he could. She missed the heat from his body and scooted closer. She rolled to face him. "Hey."

Turning his head, he raised his brows in question.

"I don't know if I ever said thanks."

He looked away. "It's nothing."

That struck a nerve. "It's not nothing, unless my life and sanity are nothing."

"No, that's not what I meant." Rolling toward her, JC pulled the blanket up on their shoulders. "I meant it's no big deal. I mean, well, anyone would have helped."

"No, they wouldn't. No one else was digging for me but you. I admit I didn't want you along at first, but I'm glad you're here." Her face was inches from his, and she suddenly wanted to kiss him and hug him tightly. She held back. Surely, the fear of losing Crystal, and all the death and loss she'd witnessed, was playing on her emotions. Once she found Crystal, JC would go his own way again and she wouldn't miss him.

"I'm glad I heard you calling out." Something dark passed over his eyes and he closed them.

"How did you get out of your apartment without getting hurt?"

He was quiet so long she thought he'd gone to sleep. "I wasn't home. I partied with some friends the night before and was too drunk to go home. So I wasn't there when it hit."

She bit her lip, remembering now he'd said he wasn't there. No wonder he'd been so desperate to get to her. He felt guilty about his family.

"They were in the front doorway, or where the door would have been. Mom probably kept Kaylee there because they say that's where it's safest. But that doesn't help if the building collapses." He drew in a ragged breath and she cupped her palm to his cheek. Her fingers felt dampness on his skin.

He lay there, eyes closed, unspeaking for a bit, then took another breath. "But I wasn't too late to save you."

"No, you weren't. You saved my life, JC." Niki listened to his ragged breaths, keeping her hand to his face as she fell asleep.

Chapter Eight

When Niki woke, pale sunlight battled the mist off the lake and she shivered against the damp cold. She realized she was alone under the blanket and left the tent to look for JC and Antwon.

The fire had been built up, the wall of rocks around it taller but there was no sign of the guys. Once again, they had slipped away while she slept. Zipping her coat, she went in search of the toilets and shower stalls. She found a line, and discovered the number of people staying at the lake had grown. Campsites crowded against campsites. People even camped in their vehicles in the parking lot.

As she waited in line, she listened to the conversations around her.

"We came from Santa Maria. They're telling everyone to get off the coast, over the mountains. A volcano has risen in the ocean off Santa Barbara."

"There wasn't even an island there, and suddenly this volcano came up out of the ocean."

"…could erupt at any time."

"…warnings of another tidal wave. If the coast

doesn't fall into the ocean, the ocean will swallow it up."

Crystal. She had to believe the Farmers escaped the first tsunami and were safely east of the coastal mountains. She spoke to the woman in front of her who held the hand of a young boy. "Are the phones working yet?"

The woman shook her head. "Mine isn't. There's no telling when the cell towers will be repaired. I imagine ones far from the city like this will be further down the list."

After cleaning up as best she could in the sink and drinking the ice cold water cupped in her hand, Niki went back to their camp. There was no sign of the guys. Her breath caught in her throat, her stomach tightened as a wave of panic hit. Nothing would happen to them. She was acting like a baby. She hadn't needed anyone in her life before the earthquake, she would get by somehow. Surrounded by people at the lake, nothing bad could happen. She could stay there and survive on fish until she found a way to get to Crystal.

Grabbing one of Antwon's sharp sticks, she walked to the water's edge. She'd never fished before, not even with a pole. The odds of her catching one with a stick were slim to joking. But she had to try. She took off her shoes and socks, rolled up her pants and waded into the shallow, icy water. Standing still, she waited, searching through the water plants for movement.

Soon she realized the fish were there, but not moving, much like she was. Each time she thrust and missed, they swam away and she had to wade a bit farther out. Her legs were growing numb by the time she caught one.

Her hands were shaky from the lack of food, so she made her way to shore. After eating, she could catch more and cook them for the guys to eat when they got back.

A few hours later she had eaten, fished again and cooked her catch and she was still alone. She wandered the grounds for a while, taking in the activity. Some of those who came during the morning had supplies enough to share. People banded together to cook rice and beans, and passed out small servings of food and water in paper cups and bowls.

Niki found herself holding a trash bag and helped keep waste under control. It felt good to be doing something productive, something besides worrying about Crystal. And wondering if JC was coming back.

At one point, the slowdown after the lunch rush, as she would've called it at the Taco Shack, she saw Anne standing off to one side of the eating area. The ghost smiled and waved, and was gone. This time it struck Niki as comforting, a friend waving hello in passing. She made her way back to her camp, spread one of the blankets and wrapped herself in it to take a nap. Sleeping in the tent in the crowded campground had been disruptive, with her waking often to burrow closer to JC. Sometime during the night, he'd wrapped an arm around her and pulled her tightly against him. She'd slept quietly after that.

Using Antwon's blanket for a pillow, she lay on her side and stared at the green tent wall. Where had JC gone? And why did it matter so much that he wasn't there?

She'd broken up with her last boyfriend over a year ago, if she stretched the meaning of the word boyfriend. He wanted more sex than she was willing to give. He'd been sweet enough at the start. Dates to the movies or a party. Dinners at inexpensive restaurants. They'd been comfortable together, but it eventually sank into her head that the dates were just another chance for him to try to have sex. It had become clear there was no love involved. Even on her end.

Sometimes she thought the only person she had ever loved, could ever love, was Crystal. Well, and Lisa. *At least that proves I can love.*

She shivered, the blanket only barely keeping away the cold. She missed her lumpy old sagging mattress and thick comforter. Her pillow. She missed her space heater. Hot coffee.

She missed JC. Where did he go?

The tent grew blurry and she realized her eyes were watering. She wasn't crying. Not really. The cold made them water, that's all it was. A tear escaped, followed by a sob. Too much had happened in the last few days. Her chest felt heavy, making breathing difficult. She gulped in air. Then let go and let the tears fall until she fell asleep.

~*~

A firm hand shook her shoulder and Niki tried to waken from the deep fog that held her. Visions of her apartment walls falling around her, of Anne's black safety-soled shoes poking out from beneath a trash bag, of neighborhoods flattened to rubble, poured through her mind. "No, please, God, no."

"Hey, Mouse, wake up." JC jerked at her shoulder again. "Look what we got."

As the sound of his voice cut through her nightmare, she sat up and grabbed him in a tight hug. "I thought you were gone."

His arms tightened around her. He stroked her hair and whispered shushing noises. "Hey, it's okay. You're okay."

Realizing she was clinging to him, she pulled back, hot with embarrassment. "Sorry. I was having a bad dream."

"This should help." He stood, pulling her arm to follow. Three sleeping bags were rolled up in the corner next to a pile of clothes. As she turned to JC, she noticed folding chairs outside the tent near the fire. "This is awesome! How'd you do it? Where'd you get it all?"

He led her to a chair and sat next to her. "We went to Taft. The cops have better things to do than keep the stores from being robbed, and the merchants agreed people need the stuff to survive, so they're giving stuff away. We got food, clothes, water, all sorts of stuff. We got as much as the milk crates would hold."

"Do you think we can ride back to the coast, one day? Find Crystal."

His jaw tightened. "Um, Mouse—I mean Niki— about that..."

"They evacuated the coast," she filled in.

He caught her eye, surprise on his face. "Yeah. You heard. Most likely she came through Taft on her way to Bakersfield. There's a message board at the refugee center where people are leaving their names so family knows they're okay, in addition to the lists the authorities are keeping. I put yours up there. I didn't see hers."

She closed her eyes and prayed, for Crystal's life and her own sanity. *Please, God, let her be safe.* She heard movement and JC's voice sounded close.

"We'll find her. Whatever it takes, we'll find your sister."

Antwon stuck his head inside the tent. "Where'd you put the food, man? I'm hungry."

JC pointed to the two milk crates. "I figured we

wanted them inside the tent to keep them safe." He grabbed the box on top of one and handed Niki a granola bar. "You need to eat."

"Thanks." She tore into it, the sweetness delighting her taste buds. "Chocolate. This is so good. I had rice and beans with the other campers while you were gone, and I caught a fish for breakfast. I miss real food. Seasonings. I'd kill for some taco sauce."

Tugging at a lock of her hair, JC said, "I'll try to find some next time we're in town."

The people at the lake were getting organized as more people came with supplies. Many had to leave behind houses that were unsafe to live in, but standing. They'd been able to take pots and pans, silverware, bedding. Others waited in line at the big box stores in Bakersfield for whatever they could get, including canned goods.

An area was set up as a community kitchen, with a large bonfire off to one side where big pots of water continually boiled. Propane stoves and barbeque grills for cooking lined a folding banquet table. Washtubs sat on folding tables for washing up, alongside giant bottles of hand sanitizer. Hygiene became of major importance as reality set in. If help was coming, it was a long way off. They needed to do all they could to prevent illness.

As the days passed, Niki got to know more of the people at the lake. She sat with the women in between shifts in the kitchen, where she had taken to coordinating the schedules and organizing meals and supplies. As she listened to one young mother talk, she noticed a small boy standing behind the woman. Or rather, the ghost of a small boy.

The mother was talking about her son. "He was such an angel, all love and kisses, never a bad spell."

The boy looked at Niki. "Tell her I'm here."

She opened her mouth to speak before thinking. "Did he have curly brown hair like yours?"

His mother smiled. "Yes. It always needed brushing."

"Tell her," the child insisted.

I can't, she thought. Tell a mother she saw the ghost of her child? She couldn't upset the woman like that.

"Mom needs to know I'm okay."

All right. It took all her nerve to speak. "He's here. Behind you."

The woman jumped in her seat and twisted to look around. "What? How can he be?"

"He wants you to know he's all right."

Whispers snaked around their circle as the women spoke behind their hands, looking at Niki.

Tears ran down the mother's cheeks. "What are you saying?"

Niki fought her own tears, feeling the woman's pain. "I'm sorry. I didn't want to say anything but he insisted."

The boy moved beside his mom, put his hand on hers in her lap, and spoke to Niki. The woman glanced down at her leg as if she felt his presence.

"His hand is on yours. He says it was his time. That he had come here to learn love and be your child." Niki knotted her own hands in her lap. This was crazy. She was talking to a ghost, and talking to the ghost's mom.

"Did— was he in pain for long?"

The boy shook his head. Niki said, "He says he went fast. No pain."

He began to fade.

"He says he has to go now. He only wanted you to know he loves you and he's okay."

The mother smiled through her tears. "Thank you, Niki, this was a wonderful gift. If you'll excuse me, I need to go find my husband."

The woman walked away. Niki sat for a moment, then went in search of JC. He was tinkering under the hood of her car, which he and Antwon had towed to the lake with the use of a truck and some rope. He'd taken out the radiator and was working on straightening the frame. The old Chevy needed some body work, and he said he'd have to drain the oil and fuel to get the water out, but he thought he could get it running.

"Can I talk to you for a minute?" she asked.

"Sure." He leaned one hip against the grill. "What's up?"

"I saw another ghost."

"How do you know it was a ghost? Was it someone you know?"

She flung her arms around, searching for words to explain it all. "No, a little boy. He was standing by his mom when she was telling us about him. He died in the quake."

"How did you know it was her kid?"

"I asked his mom."

JC raised an eyebrow. "You told her you saw her son?"

He thought she was crazy, too. Cool—not. "I didn't know what else to do. The boy told me to tell her he was okay."

"So he talked to you, too."

"You don't believe me, do you?" Why had she thought he would? Maybe she had been building their friendship out of proportion in her head.

"I didn't say that. I've just never known anyone who talked to the dead before." He pulled off his beanie and scratched his head before putting it back on.

"I don't talk to the dead. Do I? I mean, it was only

this one kid, not a ton of dead people. But I had to tell you about it. I thought you'd help me understand it."

After wiping the grease off his hands with an old t-shirt, JC took her hand. "I want to help you, but I don't know anything about this kind of stuff. What do you think it means?"

She squeezed his fingers, enjoying the warmth, the connection. It seemed like only when she was close to him she remembered she was alive, not wandering in limbo. "I don't know. I've seen Anne a few more times, too."

"Does she talk to you?"

"No, she smiles and waves and then disappears."

He shrugged. "So maybe she's saying she's okay, too."

"I guess so. I wish I knew for sure."

He dropped her hand and looked under the car's hood. "Can you hand me that socket extension?"

When she bent over, the sweat pants she wore, which were a size too big, rode low on her hips and threatened to slide off. She yanked them up as she straightened, the tool in her hand.

JC grinned at her. "You need a belt for those things."

"No kidding." She felt the warmth of embarrassment wash over her as she handed him the extension.

"Thanks." He fiddled with the wrench, then threw her a glance before reaching into the depths of the engine. "So what's with the tattoo?"

"What tattoo?" She only had one. She was stalling, trying to think of an answer, how much to admit.

"The one on your, um, hip. The broken heart. I, uh, noticed it when you crawled out of your apartment."

Crap, that meant he'd seen her naked ass. Heat crawled up her neck. The tattoo sat low on her lower back, half a heart with a jagged edge. The only person who knew what it meant was Crystal. She was too afraid others would laugh at her, so she never explained. But this was JC. He'd understand. "You know those necklaces and bracelets that girls get? It's a heart in two pieces that fit together. Each piece is on a separate necklace or bracelet."

He continued to work in silence, so she wasn't even sure he was listening. She took a breath and continued. "You get the necklaces with your best friend and each of you wears one. It's as if she's the other half of your heart. Best friends forever."

When she didn't say more, he stopped working and looked at her. She chewed on her bottom lip. "I never had a best friend. I always felt like I only had half a heart. So I got the tattoo."

"I'm sorry. I guess I shouldn't have asked." He wiped his hands on the rag and stepped closer. "I'm sorry you never had a best friend."

She laughed. "I survived. The tattoo seems kind of silly now."

"No, not silly. It had meaning to you when you did it." He took a lock of her hair and twirled it around his fingers.

"I guess."

"If it makes you feel better, I'll show you my tats."

Naughty thoughts flashed through her mind too quickly to pin down, pooling in a hot puddle somewhere low inside her. She fought the urge not to squirm. "I know you have the tribal on your arm, and the knuckle tats. There are others?"

"Other."

"Okay, then. I'm waiting." She folded her arms across her chest and leaned on one leg.

His dark eyes pierced hers as he unzipped the

hoodie and slipped it off, dropping it on the car's grill. In one move, he yanked the two layers of shirts over his head and dropped them, too.

Niki first noticed the muscles…everywhere. Hard, toned, and perfect, clear down to his drooping waistband and the dark arrow of hair there. Swallowing, she brought her eyes back up to the colors on his chest.

A large dragon hung in midair, pointed tail curved below, rear feet splayed. Its pale green wings spread across JC's ripped chest. Fierce teeth were sharp against the orange flames shooting from its mouth.

And in its front claws, deep crimson and dripping blood, was half a heart, with a torn, jagged edge.

It took a moment for Niki to realize she'd stopped breathing. Not only did he have a jagged heart tat, but it was the opposite half to hers. *Crazy.* When she heard her whispered response, she wasn't sure if she meant his tattoo or the synchronicity. "That's really cool."

He grunted, then pulled his shirts and hoodie back on.

"Why'd you get yours?" Half of her wanted to hear some magical answer, like he was looking for his other half like she was, but she knew guys didn't talk like that.

"I don't know. I saw one like it with an eagle instead of the dragon and thought it fit me. But a dragon is even stronger than an eagle, ya know?"

"Yeah, I get what you mean, JC. And a dragon suits you." If it weren't for his strength, she would have fallen apart so many times since they'd teamed up.

Chapter Nine

The ground shook, waking Niki. JC's arm tightened around her as he rolled over her to protect her. She cried out, "What's happening?"

Both JC and Antwon answered her. "Earthquake."

The rolling waves of seismic energy continued as if sifting the chaff from the wheat, or the silt from gold. Niki prayed silently for it to end. Only when it stopped did she relax again and squirm out from under JC. "I didn't think it would quit."

"I know. That one was huge, like the first one. Thank goodness these tents bend with the motion."

"I wonder how much damage they got to the pipeline," Antwon said.

For the past two months he and JC had worked at Occidental Petroleum in Elk Hills, where they were repairing oil and natural gas lines. Once the leaks were repaired, the local refineries could begin production again, providing fuel locally, if not on a larger scale.

Climbing from his sleeping bag, Antwon pulled his jeans on over his boxers. Tucking in the shirt he'd slept in, he grabbed his jacket and went outside.

"I should go, too. See what everyone says." JC stuck his feet into his shoes, grabbed his hoodie and followed Antwon, wearing the sweat pants he slept in.

Niki pulled her hairbrush out of her backpack and began brushing her hair. In the past week, they'd had increasingly large aftershocks, and some speculated they were actually a warning of the volcano getting ready to blow. It was only a matter of time, they said. She feared the strength of this morning's quake meant the volcano had finally erupted.

She tried to put the volcano out of her head. No one was living on the coast, so Crystal was safe, somewhere. Niki needed to travel to Lost Hills, to the north, and check their refugee lists. And if Crystal wasn't on them, head south to Santa Clarita and look. She would find her sister, no matter how long it took.

After putting on her jeans, she folded the three sleeping bags. JC's carried his clean, earthy scent, filling her with comfort. His presence was becoming necessary to her. He was so different than she had imagined him from the few impressions she'd had in school. He and his bros looked like they'd walked out of an Eminem music video, and she had written JC off as a wild druggie like his friends. She really felt awful about her judgments, as she learned what was important to him. Most important was his need for family.

She had finally seen both of his hands one day and was able to make out the knuckle tattoos. *Familia*, with a heart and cross on the left pinky. Spanish for family. She'd asked him why he chose that word.

"I dunno. Tattoos are supposed to be about what's important to you. So I picked family."

"Is that why you still lived at home? To be close to

them?" she'd asked.

"I guess. Mom's job didn't pay much. She worked part time at the school so she could be home with Kaylee. So I paid rent and bought groceries to help out."

Another light dawned for Niki. "You rode a bike around town. So your mom could have the car?"

JC tugged at his knit cap, which she'd come to recognize as a sign he wasn't comfortable talking. "No. Kaylee's dad took the car when he left and we rode the bus. Or Mom and Kaylee did. I rode my bike as part of my workout, killing two birds."

She'd stopped asking questions then, to quit putting him on the spot. In another world, the pre-apocalypse world, she might have taken these parts of JC as wonderful signs of the father of her future kids, if she ever planned to have them. But kids needed love. She would love Crystal's children, she was sure. So maybe she'd be the best-damned aunt any kid ever had. Family wasn't something she aspired to have.

Good thing, she supposed, with the way life was looking. How much more painful would the chaos around them be if she had to watch her children suffer? Her sister's kids? Or have to see them die.

The zipper on the tent flap opened and JC entered, avoiding eye contact. Her stomach clenched. He had bad news.

"That was the volcano we felt. Caleb heard the report on his two-way radio. There are reports of landslides along the coastal mountains. Basically flattening the range along the coast. If the cities didn't drop below sea level already, the tidal wave they're expecting might swallow the land."

The CB radios in the camp were the new place to get news, with a channel dedicated to updates. But the updates always seemed so minor. No one was able to explain why, after two months, there was no electricity, supplies like food and water weren't being brought in. The closest explanation was that the supplies were all needed locally. Even the largest cities were too busy helping themselves to help anyone else.

Niki's eyes widened as she listened to JC. When she was little, her parents joked about Bakersfield becoming beachfront property when the Big One hit. Even as a kid she'd never imagined it would come to pass. "How... how far inland will the water come?"

"No one here knows for sure. A lot of it depends on how much of the mountains remain. But the valley that Taft is in, Maricopa, McKittrick, they should be okay. And we're safe here."

She rushed the few steps to him and wrapped her arms tightly around him, burying her face in his shirt. He didn't mention Crystal, but she knew he knew she was even more worried now. The frustration of not being able to find her sister ate at her daily, sometimes round-the-clock.

JC stroked her hair, running his hand over the back of her head. "It'll be okay. Somehow it'll all be okay."

Lifting her head, she looked up at him, wondering if he really believed it or if he just wanted to calm her. His eyes were intense on her, gold flecks sparkling in the sea of brown, so much emotion boiling in their depths. She wished he'd say what he felt so she didn't always wonder.

Her gaze shifted to his lips with a sudden need to feel them on hers. She licked her bottom lip, debating kissing him to see what he'd do. As she thought it, his mouth came to hers and captured her soul.

He tasted of mint, like the gum he chewed, and of hidden passion. His hand on the back of her head held her firmly, supporting, not imprisoning. Pressed against the length of him, she felt her body molding around him, to fit as comfortably as her favorite pair of jeans.

How long she kissed him, she wasn't sure, but her heart pounded in her ears and she gasped for air when he pulled away, holding her close. He rested his forehead on hers, eyes closed, saying nothing.

And she found she didn't need words. His heart spoke to hers and calmed her. Whatever lay ahead, he'd be there.

~*~

While the guys worked in the oilfields, Niki did what she could to stay busy. They'd taken the dirt bikes, so she had to remain at the lake. During meal times she helped the other women cook, or washed dishes in the large pots of scalding water. But in between meals, the hours dragged.

She sat on a rock next to the lake, staring into the sunlight reflected off the water. The light was blinding, but the heat of the sun on her face seemed purifying, somehow. One of her foster moms had taken her to a dermatologist a few times and he'd used a sun lamp on her face to clear her acne. This felt the same. Gentle heat that somehow lifted her mood.

Allowing herself to focus on the lapping water rather than her stampeding worries, she took in a deep breath and let it out slowly. She felt so peaceful.

Anne's voice spoke to her. "Finally. I've been shouting to you for months."

Niki blinked and sat straighter, looking around her. Anne's ghost, wearing a lime green bikini, sat on a towel on the shore beside Niki.

"The sun feels great, doesn't it?" Anne lifted her face

up to the rays.

"Yeah, I guess. What are you doing here?"

"I don't work today so I thought we could hang out."

"Very funny." Niki closed her eyes for a moment before opening them again to see if Anne was still there.

"I'm not going anywhere. Not while you still need me."

"But, you're already gone. Aren't you supposed to go to the light or something?" Now she was sure she had lost whatever sanity she'd clung to growing up.

"I'm not trapped. I can come and go. I'm here to help you learn to use your gift."

Niki shook her head. "What gift?"

"This one. You see dead people."

"So I noticed. What's up with that?" If that was a gift, she wondered if she could exchange it for something more useful, like the ability to see the future. Then she'd know what to do to keep them safe.

"There will be more. It might not seem like much, but you can give the survivors some comfort. Just do what you did before. I'll help when I can."

"But why—" When Niki looked back at the shore, Anne was gone. A hollow ache hit Niki's stomach. She got up and walked toward the kitchen area to see if she could help get dinner going.

~*~

After two days they felt it was safe enough to drive west on the dirt bikes and survey the damage from the tidal wave. Every trip the guys took, they searched for vehicles from which they could siphon gas, but it was getting harder and harder to find ones that hadn't already been drained. At some point, they would need to find some other means of transportation.

The trees around the houses in Dustin Acres were beginning to bud. March was too early to call spring in the past, but everyone had begun to notice the days were already growing hotter. Summertime was going to be unbearable, at this rate.

Two miles west of Taft, on a dirt road paved by the traffic drawn by the appearance of a new volcano, the three of them stood on the rocky shoreline of California. The new coast. No lush sands, no lifeguard stations, only water and sea gulls. In the distance Niki heard the cry of a sea lion but couldn't distinguish the animal from the rocks.

"This is crazy." Antwon said what Niki was thinking.

"No shit," JC agreed.

Someone should have made smartass remarks, the way people always did when they joked about California falling into the ocean. But it was no longer funny. Staring out at the water, Niki observed the black tower of smoke emanating from the volcano now named San Bruno. To the south of it were the Channel Islands, now taller than before, almost forming one large island.

She'd been told all of this by people at the lake, but seeing it brought on the final shock value. Her stomach knotted and acid filled the twisted space. There was no going back. They would never recreate the cities that had been, even the ones not under water. Life might go on but it would never resemble what she knew as normal.

Antwon broke into her thoughts. "Hey, JC. Almost forgot. My foreman said they're going to start tearing down the old company housing in Fellows and put up new homes. No more tent cities."

"Really?" Hopeful butterflies in Niki's stomach began emerging from their cocoons. A real house.

"Yeah. I heard that they're making mini-communities in all the cities. Housing, schools and a community kitchen all together. The big companies will build them for their employees' families. And the cities are building others. Oxy is already breaking ground in Fellows, so JC and I will be able to get houses or apartments or whatever they're building, as soon as they're done."

JC caught her eye, staring meaningfully at her, and she wondered what he meant. *Use your words*, she wanted to yell. Would he want her to move with him?

The thought surprised her. She'd never considered moving in with a guy. The joy she'd felt moving out of a foster home and into an apartment of her own, paid for with her own earnings, was unmatchable. The feeling hadn't diminished in the eight months she lived there. It didn't matter that the walls were so thin she could hear her neighbors breathe, or that she had to regularly replace the roach traps. Well, that did matter, but she knew someday, with another promotion, she would have been able to move somewhere nicer. And she wouldn't need a roommate to get her there.

She suddenly realized JC might not want to share a place with her. Without thinking, she shifted closer to JC, and when his arm wrapped around her waist, she sighed in relief. Sometimes she could never be close enough to him.

Part of her worried she was clinging to him after losing so much at once. He'd been her savior, pulled her from the bowels of her apartment. What if her feelings were simply hero worship? Her attraction to her crushes in the past always faded eventually. Except for Adam Levine of the band Maroon 5. That crush wasn't going anywhere. If she moved in with JC, she was afraid her attraction to him might fade, too.

Resting her head on his shoulder, she let the sound of the rolling waves comfort her. She lived in a tent and wore clothes donated by strangers. Her only possession, a beat up thirty-something-year-old Chevy, sat by the lake awaiting a radiator transplant. When you had nothing, you had nothing to lose. If JC asked her to share an apartment, she would say yes.

Antwon walked back toward the dirt bikes. "I'm going to see some friends in Bako. I'll catch you guys later tonight."

Niki waved good-bye and turned back to JC. "That's cool you might have a place to live soon."

"Yeah. It'll be good to get closer to normal."

"No kidding. I never imagined my life could change so drastically."

JC brushed her hair back from her face. "I know. I used to imagine this…"

When he didn't continue, she pushed. "What, a big earthquake changing the world?"

His eyes softened, darkened, and his hand cupped her cheek. His lips thinned before he spoke. "No. I imagined kissing you. And you, kissing me back."

She blinked. "When?"

He looked out over the ocean. "In high school."

"But you didn't know me in high school."

"I wanted to. But we didn't have any classes together. I didn't know how to talk to you."

"You guys laughed at me in the halls between classes," she said. "And called me Mouse. You smooshed stinky cheese through the vents in my locker."

"They laughed. And did the cheese. I should've stopped them. I know. But I didn't know how."

"You could have talked to me. I'm not a total bitch."

Or was she? Her anger at the world took up most of her being until everything changed so much. "Well, maybe not. I guess it's good you didn't try. I hated everything back then."

"I heard you got bounced around a lot in foster homes." He rested his arms on her shoulders, his lower half pressing against hers.

"I deserved it. If I ever find the Farmers, I need to apologize. They tried to love me."

"You're different now," he said. "When you didn't want me to go along with you after the first earthquake, I thought maybe you still thought I was an ass. I was so scared you'd shut me out."

Her lips twisted into a wry smile. "I wanted to. All I could think about was Crystal. I couldn't understand why you wouldn't go away. But even before we reached the 101, I was glad you were with me. I don't think I could have survived all this without you."

"Yeah, you would have. You're a fighter. Just took you a while to see what was worth fighting against." He kissed her, gently but confidently. His hands held her face, then her shoulders, and travelled down her back as if uncertain where to land.

She stretched on her toes to meet him as fireworks shot through her body. Her palms pressed against his hard chest, trapped between them, feeling his heartbeat pounding hard. Her pulse echoed his in her ears.

When JC finally broke the kiss, he held her in his arms a while longer, both of them watching the seagulls dive into the cresting waves as if their world never missed a beat. Finally, he said, "We should get back."

"Can we stop by the refugee center on the way to the lake?"

"Of course."

Niki checked the job board at the center, scanning job titles for something she could do, while JC wandered off. At the lake, she helped out in the community kitchen to earn their portion of the food prepared each day. Paying jobs were few, with most people earning credits for supplies, or housing when it became available. She didn't understand why the electrical plants hadn't been repaired in two and a half months. Why the wind turbines in the mountains weren't powering the cities nearby. This was America, not some Third World country without the means to recover from so much devastation.

With JC and Antwon getting on the list for housing in Fellows, she needed to plan a future. There had to be some kind of job she could do, some way she could contribute to the rebuilding of the area.

Her attention was drawn to a girl with pale blonde hair standing at the opposite end of the board. She looked familiar—Sharon, no Sherry. Crystal's friend from Santa Maria. Niki's pulse jumped in excitement.

"Sherry? Is that you?"

The girl tossed her ponytail over her shoulder and looked down the board. "Yeah. Oh my God, you're Crystal's sister aren't you? I'm so sorry."

Niki's blood drained from her body. "For...for what?"

"Um, your sister? I'm so sad she's gone."

Gone. Niki reached for the board to steady herself but it was no good. Her knees began to give out.

JC appeared from nowhere and caught her before she hit the sidewalk. "Mouse! What's wrong?"

"I'm so sorry, I thought she knew," Sherry said, her eyes welling with tears.

"Crystal." Niki could only whisper the name.

"You know her sister?" JC asked Sherry.

"Yes, she lived down the street from me. When we got the call to evacuate, my family drove past their house. They were getting into their car. It seemed like only a minute later the water hit. My dad had to floor it to get to the freeway. We ran from there up the hillside. The next day when the water went down we went back to our house. The Farmers' car was upside down at the end of our street, maybe half a mile in the wrong direction." She burst into tears.

Niki sat in JC's embrace as ice coursed through her body. No way could Crystal be gone. She'd feel it. She'd know it.

Sherry gulped a few breaths, then continued. Listening numbly, Niki heard Sherry explain about checking the refugee lists looking for her neighbors. "I never saw her name."

Neither had Niki. She looked over her shoulder at JC. "It can't be true," she whispered.

His eyes glassed over and welled with the tears Niki couldn't shed. "I'm sorry. I'm so sorry." He kissed her head and continued to mumble his sorrow between sniffles.

His pain made Niki's that much sharper, which confused her even more. It was her sister. She should be the one crying, not him. But she couldn't feel anything beyond the stabbing in her heart. Icy shards formed, hardened, stealing her warmth.

"I need to go home," she told JC. "Please take me home."

Chapter Ten

A week later, Niki sat in a large tent in Taft listening with half an ear to the Planning Committee speaker. Partly because of all the chaotic energy emanating from the people around her, and partly from her racing thoughts, she couldn't focus. Crystal's name hadn't shown up on any of the survivor lists, not in Taft or in Bako. She continued to hold onto hope her sister survived, in spite of what Sherry had said. Not many new names were added to the lists each week. Communication between Bakersfield, Taft and Lost Hills had improved and their lists were finally coordinated. There were times she needed to see for herself and would talk JC into going with her on the dirt bike to check the ones in the other cities.

Population at Buena Vista Lake was growing. Refugees of Santa Maria, Paso Robles and the surrounding communities blended in with the residents of Lost Hills, Taft, Bakersfield and Wasco. The need for housing and food overwhelmed the supplies that had been brought in. The government agencies in charge of disasters said their stores had run out. Locally, the fields that normally grew crops like cotton and sugar beets were planted with a variety of vegetables, including soy beans for protein. Today the Planning Committee was announcing the latest news from the EPA about the toxic gasses emitted by the San Bruno volcano, and a new volcano about to erupt near Yosemite.

The officials who spoke at these meetings could put a hyperactive twelve-year-old to sleep. They used the largest—probably made up—words possible, and combined them with as many unnecessary words as they could, as if the truth needed to be kept from the community. It frustrated her to no end to leave these planning sessions more confused than when she came.

As she finally made her way out of the large tent at the end, an older couple approached. "Are you Niki?"

"Yes."

"My sister told me to find you," the woman said. "She was one of the lake people for a short time. You— you helped her."

Niki knew what the woman meant. Everybody thanked her for helping them heal after she told them about their dead loved ones.

"I was wondering…" the woman's words drifted off as if uncertain how to ask.

Closing her eyes a moment, Niki called to Anne in her mind. *Are this woman's loved ones here?* When she opened her eyes, an entire extended family shimmered behind the couple. So many lost! Grief swallowed Niki and she fought her way above it. She drew in a breath of cool air and blinked tears away as she met the old woman's eyes. Her voice rasped through the thickness of her throat. "You lost a lot of family."

The woman brought a tissue to her eyes and nodded. Her husband pulled a handkerchief from his pocket.

"I'm sorry," Niki said, clearing her throat, and laughed at her sudden urge to run and hide. "I'm new to this. I don't know how to shut off the emotion. There's so much love pouring from them it spills past you and into me."

She went on to describe whom she saw, the baby with two bottom teeth, and an older man with a cane. All huddled together as if for a Christmas photo. "They are all glowing in golden light. I think that's love."

When she finished talking to the couple and their family faded away, she needed to sit down, needed to be alone. She was so drained. Seeing dead people was definitely something she hadn't learned how to cope with while working at the Taco Shack.

Finding a tree in the park, she sank to the ground and leaned against the rough bark. This part of life continued. The trees, the pale grass trying to survive in the early spring warming sun. This hadn't changed. She tried to let the sadness of that couple's loss drain out of her and into the ground.

In her mind she welcomed Anne, having come to cherish their conversations so like the ones on their breaks at work. "That one was so hard to get through," she told her friend in her thoughts.

"You need to learn to block the emotion. You don't have to feel it. You can see it and tell others that it's there," Anne said.

"See it? How?"

Anne began to shimmer with golden light. "This is God's love, universal love. You had it right when you told that couple about the love being sent to them."

She took on a pink hue. "This is the love between couples, romantic love, the kind that soul mates have." She continued to take on different shades and told Niki what they meant.

Niki hoped she could remember it all.

"Don't worry," Anne reassured her with a laugh. "You won't be quizzed at the end of the supervisor's meeting. Tell the people what you feel. But feel it dispassionately. Don't take on their emotions."

Before Niki could ask what that meant, she felt JC kneel beside her. She opened her eyes and smiled. "I knew it was you."

"Do I smell that bad? I can't wash up till we get back to the lake." His clothes were covered with dust and oil.

"No, silly. I could feel your energy. Anne was teaching me to feel the emotions of the ghosts. No, not to feel their emotions but recognize them so I can tell their loved ones."

He looked as confused as she felt. "Just don't let them drain you. You get so washed out after talking to people, sometimes."

Rolling to her feet, she agreed. "Anne's trying to teach me how to do it without getting so tired."

JC put a small packet in her hand, wrapping her fingers around it. "I found this for you."

She opened her fingers and saw her favorite sour candies. "Oh. My. God. Where did you get this?"

"One of the guys bought them at a big box store in Bako. He was selling them at lunch."

Popping a piece on her tongue, she savored the mouth-watering sour sugar coating that melted away, leaving sweet chewy candy. "Oh, this is so good. Here." She put a piece in his mouth and watched him pucker.

They laughed at the simple pleasure, taking turns feeding each other as they walked to the parking lot where his dirt bike sat. He'd found a pair of helmets a few weeks back, and they pulled them on while talking about their day.

"What's JC stand for?" she asked, suddenly curious.

"Jordan Christopher."

"That's a nice name. Jordan. A strong name."

Riding behind JC, she loved the feel of his strong body when she wrapped herself tightly around him, her hands tucked into the pockets of his hoodie. She missed the days before the helmet when she could rest her face on his back. Slender as he was, he was large enough to cut the cold wind as they rode, blocking it from her and keeping her warm.

After eating in the kitchen at the lake, they went back to their tent and turned on the battery-operated lantern, sitting close together on their sleeping bags. JC spoke first. "I want to go to Bakersfield."

"We can go on your day off."

"No, that's not what I mean. I don't know if I want to live in Fellows."

She rearranged herself on her sleeping bag so she could see him. "But that's the only housing Oxy offers. Will they pay you the difference if you want to find your own housing?"

"I don't know." He stretched out his fingers, then curled them again and turned his fists so the tats faced him. *Familia.*

Was he missing his family? She never thought to ask Anne why his mom and sister never appeared to her. "Do you miss them?"

"Yeah."

"I can't imagine." She stretched out and rested her head on his thigh, feeling the rough warmth of the fabric against her cheek. "Do you want to talk about them?"

"Nah." He continued to flex and curl his fingers

distractedly.

"I saw you and Kaylee at the playground once. I was sitting by the pool, heard her laughter, and had to watch you two. I couldn't make out what you said that had her laughing so hard."

"It didn't take much. I used to call her Miss Giggles." He sighed and his hands stopped clenching. "I need to go there."

"Where? To the playground?"

He stretched out to lie beside her, his face inches from hers. "No. I don't know where exactly. It's like my family is calling me to come home."

"I still haven't found a job I can do."

His smile was distant. "Something will come along. You help out a lot here. Keep the kitchen going so everyone can eat."

Her stomach felt hollow. Was the attraction between them wearing thin already? Once, he made it sound like he rescued her because he couldn't rescue his family. Like he'd made her his project to keep safe. But that wasn't enough to build a relationship on. They were quite the pair. A loner and a loser, unable to love.

Her eyes burned as if she had no more tears to shed. That was probably true. She'd held off at first, not crying until she woke to find JC gone. As time passed with no word of Crystal, she'd cried more and more often. It seemed the well was running dry now that she was afraid she and JC were growing apart.

He'd never asked her to move in with him when he got a place in Fellows. Had she just assumed it would happen? She couldn't recall any clear conversations they'd had about it. And now he wanted to go back to Bakersfield. If he did, she could always go to Lisa, see if she could help Niki find a job. "Um, JC? We need to talk."

He met her gaze. "What's up?"

"It's about me working in the kitchen."

"You don't want to work in the kitchen? Take one of the other jobs on the boards in Taft. It's not like you're signing on to work there for life. You can change jobs if something better comes along."

"No, that's not it. I like working in the kitchen. I know what I'm doing there. It's more of the same. Same as before, you know? I need something the same. It's like nothing about my life is, except my name."

JC took her hand and wove his fingers between hers. "Some of the different is good though, right?"

She laughed in relief and kissed the back of his hand. "Yeah, JC. Some of it's real good."

"That's cool." Cupping his hand behind her neck, he pulled her to him and kissed her hard. He broke away from her lips and kissed her cheek, and down to her neck, nipping at her skin there. Shivers rolled out from every inch he touched.

When he rested his head on her shoulder, she wondered how different things might be if they had connected before the earthquake. When she had a home to invite him to, walls to shut out the world. Would she have let him come home with her one night, finally giving in to what her body wanted but her head refused to allow? There was no way of knowing. Maybe the lack of a private home was a good thing, forcing them to really know each other before they went further.

While she knew nothing more about what he felt about her, she felt closer to him than before she spoke up. Maybe that was what Anne had meant…feel JC's emotions and not the ghosts'. Feel her own emotions.

He was quiet so long, she thought he'd fallen asleep.

She jumped when he said, "I hear my sister sometimes."

"In your memories? I know what you mean, I hear Crystal telling me about her latest crush when she used to call me."

Leaning back, he rested his head on his hand. "No. This is different. Weird. She tells me these rhymes."

"Nursery rhymes?"

"No, like clues. I can't remember exactly how they go, but she says a line at a time. Then nothing for a few hours, or a day."

"Like what?"

"I don't know. She's talking about home, and sister. Going where the heart is."

"'Home is where the heart is,' you mean?"

"Maybe that's it. Maybe she's letting me know I'll have a home again someday. It makes me want to go back to Bakersfield, though, to search for home."

Niki had only barely begun to know the meaning of the word when hers had been destroyed. She didn't know how long it would take for her to feel safe using that word to describe her living quarters again.

Chapter Eleven

Niki rode to Bakersfield on the back of JC's dirt bike on his day off. JC brought along a bag full of stuff he'd scavenged, and hoped he could find a radiator in a salvage yard for the Chevy. He dropped Niki off at Lisa's home while he went to find one.

Lisa's husband had torn down their old house since it was too badly damaged, and salvaged the materials to build a smaller one on the old foundation. They had no power or running water, but they made do like most of their neighbors. At least Lisa and Paul had stored food and water for an emergency like this. So they had water for flushing the toilet, while everyone else had to use the outhouses the city had provided.

After being engulfed in Lisa's warm embrace, Niki prepared for the barrage of questions that usually followed, starting with, "How are things between you and JC?"

Niki hesitated. "Same old, I guess."

"What do you mean? Do you love him? Has he said he loves you?"

"He's a guy. He doesn't talk about emotions."

Lisa lowered her eyebrows and glared at Niki. "You don't talk about them either. But I know you feel them. I see what he feels for you all over his face. Why don't you see it?"

Niki didn't want to analyze it. "I don't know what love looks like. Or feels like." But that was a lie. She recognized it when she communicated with the ghosts. With JC she felt safe and secure. Only when she tried to pin things down did she begin to question what was between them. She tried putting her thoughts into words for her old boss. The words poured out, and she talked for a good twenty minutes before stopping.

With a gentle smile, Lisa handed her a cup of coffee heated on a camp stove and sat back down in the chair opposite Niki at the kitchen table. "My poor girl. You survived on your instincts all those years. It's okay to trust them in love, too."

Smiling, Niki didn't argue aloud, but when she looked where her instincts had led her, with no real friends and no family around, she wasn't so sure her instincts were on the mark. "We'll see where it goes," she finally said.

~*~

JC drove to the one salvage yard he knew was open, where he'd dealt with the owner in the past. Harry had given him a list of items to look for to use in trade for parts in Harry's yard. JC left his dirt bike in front of the office when he went inside.

"Hey, kid," Harry said when he looked up from the parts he was dismantling on the counter.

JC wondered if Harry remembered anyone's name, or just called them all "kid." "Hi. I need a radiator." He told the man the year, make and model of Niki's car.

"You're in luck. There's an old Chevy in the west corner that oughta work. You got tools?"

"Yeah, thanks." JC went out the back door and wove through the carcasses of every auto model he could name, and a few he couldn't. In high school he'd taken auto shop, and had been part of the crew who worked on a stock race car that competed at the local dirt track. Since his mom didn't own a car, that was the only way he could get any practical experience. He loved working with his hands, loved the feeling he got when he turned the key after replacing parts and heard the engine start.

Popping open the hood of the Impala, JC took out his wrench and detached the hoses where they connected to the radiator. Then he went to work on the mounting bolts, two of which were frozen. Even after spraying solvent on them, he had to work so hard he was afraid he would break his wrench before they loosened.

When he finally had the radiator free and the fan moved out of the way, he lifted it from the car. Grabbing his bag of things to swap, he went back inside. Harry liked the tail light lenses, miscellaneous bolts and driver's side mirror JC had harvested from abandoned vehicles he'd come across and was willing to trade.

With his tools in his backpack and the radiator strapped to his rear fender, JC travelled slowly back to Lisa's to get Niki, so he wouldn't lose the radiator. Niki wasn't too thrilled about sandwiching the radiator between them for the ride, but it was the only way to get it back to Buena Vista.

Lisa spoke up. "Why don't you borrow my car?"

"No, thanks." JC shook his head. They didn't need to waste her gas driving back and forth. "We'll be fine this way."

"Are you sure? I can spare it for a day or two. Or I'll

drive Niki and the radiator out for you and you don't have to bring my car back."

"Really, we're okay." He motioned for Niki to get on the bike so they could leave. He nodded good-bye to Lisa and put his helmet back on. Once Niki was settled, he drove to the cemetery that overlooked the bluffs.

They set the radiator on the ground and put their helmets nearby before JC led the way to the plain marker bearing the names of his mom and sister. The last time he came, he'd come alone, needing to keep the moment to himself. This time, with Niki beside him, he felt stronger, able to face the graves more easily.

Niki touched his arm. "They're here," she said softly.

He spun to look at her, his heart racing. "You see them? Mom and Kaylee?"

She nodded. "They're speaking, but I can't hear them."

He tilted his head and shut out his own thoughts. "I do. Mom says I'm losing too much weight, I need to eat more." That made him smile.

"Sounds like a mom."

Tugging his beanie low on his forehead, he added, "She says it's about time I talked to you, too."

Niki's eyes widened and her jaw dropped. "She knew about me? Knew who I was?"

"She caught me watching you wash your car last summer. I said I knew you from school. She said I should go talk to you. I went to the gym instead."

Niki stared at him, her mouth still slack.

He shrugged. "I was afraid you'd think I was a creepy stalker, hangin' around and watching you all the time."

Her cheeks turned pink. "All the time?"

"Well...whatever. I didn't think you'd want to talk to me." He yanked the zipper of his hoodie down. It was too hot to be wearing it.

Niki looked back toward the grave markers. "They look so happy. Peaceful. They're surrounded in gold light. That's good."

A bunch of emotions tumbled in his gut, making him feel sick. He turned on his heel and walked toward the dirt bike. Suddenly, a kid ran out from behind a tree, straight for the bike. He grabbed the handle bars and started running before jumping on and kick-starting it.

JC sprinted after him. "Get the hell off my bike!"

He heard laughter. Three other young guys ran toward the nearest exit, following JC's dirt bike. JC ran until they disappeared down the street, but he was unable to catch them. Slowing to a stop, he bent over with his hands on his knees, panting hard.

He shook his head and straightened, wiping sweat from his eyes. Niki stood where the bike had been, guarding the helmets they no longer needed, and the radiator. He couldn't meet her eyes. He'd messed up, lost their ride.

Sure, once he put the radiator in her car, they'd have it to use, but there was the problem of getting the radiator, and themselves, back to the lake.

Niki picked up the helmets by their straps when he drew near. "Do you want to go back and borrow Lisa's car?"

JC bent and grabbed the radiator. At least she made it seem like he had a choice. "I guess."

When they reached the sidewalk on Panorama Drive, he looked over the bluff to the north at the oil fields, where the pumps sat frozen in mid-stroke. "It's weird. Something out here is calling me. I wish I knew where to look."

He could pinpoint the direction the pull was coming

from. The sky was clear enough to see the mountains. Somewhere northeast of where he stood was where he was supposed to be. Over the mountain. He'd been hunting up that way so he knew there was nothing but more mountain and desert in that direction. He couldn't imagine why he'd want to go that way, but the need to find out ate at his nerves.

An hour later they knocked on Lisa's door. Her smile didn't waver as she glanced first at JC, then Niki. "Well, hello."

Niki said, "Hi again. So, can we take you up on that offer of a ride to the lake?"

Lisa tilted her head. "O…kay. Sure. Let me get my purse."

Without asking questions, Lisa popped the rear hatch of her SUV so JC could stow their gear. He climbed in the back seat and buckled up.

As they pulled away, Niki spoke. "Our bike got stolen at the cemetery. Good thing they didn't take the radiator."

Glancing at JC in the rearview mirror, Lisa asked, "Do you have anti-freeze?"

"Some. Enough for now, thanks," he answered. "I've been collecting what we need as I find it."

She smiled. "Good thinking. It makes me feel better knowing you're looking out for Niki."

He grimaced. He wasn't much good at looking out for her if he let his dirt bike get stolen. Looking out the side window, he rubbed his palms over his thighs to burn off some energy.

He went straight under the hood of Niki's car as soon as they got back to the lake. He still didn't feel like talking when they shared dinner with Antwon in the tent, and hoped Niki didn't try to make him.

She ate her meal in silence, too. The tension in the tent built until it seemed it would tear through the fabric walls.

Suddenly Antwon jumped from his chair, zipping up his jacket. "Stop! Will you two stop with the brooding and talk to each other? Yell. Scream. Throw things, I don't care, but your energy is attacking me." He stormed out of the tent.

JC set down his plate and pulled off his beanie, scrunching it up.

Niki cleared her throat. "Is everything okay? You've been funny since we left the cemetery. Well, for a few days, really."

He tossed the cap aside, then grabbed it and yanked it on his head. "I can't explain it. I gotta go. Back to Bako. I missed it, whatever I was supposed to do there."

"You can go on your next day off. Take my car."

"It won't wait. It's driving me crazy. Look at this." He held out his hands, which shook with fear or adrenaline.

"Maybe you need to burn it off. You didn't work today so you didn't get much exercise. A run around the lake might help."

He tugged off his cap again. "No. That's not it. My sister is singing some stupid song in my head, the same verse over and over, but I can't make out her words. Something about Columbus and Garces."

"Christopher Columbus and Padre Garces? Maybe she's remembering history lessons."

"No, it's something more. Something I'm supposed to get. And I don't."

She placed her hand on his arm, hoping to calm him. "You can think about it during the week and we'll go next weekend."

He bolted from his chair, tipping it over. He was out

of the tent in two steps and didn't turn to look at her as he spoke. "No. I can't wait. Don't wait up for me. I don't know when I'll be back."

Niki's Chevy started up on the first try. He let the engine run for a bit, checked the coolant level again and put on the radiator cap. He realized he hadn't asked if he could take her car, but he needed to test drive it to make sure he had everything tight before she drove it. She wouldn't be any more pissed at him than she was already.

Why girls needed to talk everything out, he'd never understand. He'd dated a few girls very briefly because of their need to question everything. "What are you thinking?" "What's on your mind?" "Do you like me?" "Do you love me?" And on and on.

The answers usually made them mad. *Nothing. Nothing. I guess.* And silence.

Niki wasn't that way, thank God, because he needed to figure this out on his own. Kaylee mentioned several locations in Bakersfield in her little rhymes. JC planned to start by visiting them to see if they gave him any clues.

He went first to Garces Circle, the roundabout on Chester Avenue with the statue of Padre Garces, one of the early pioneers of the area. He was pretty sure Kaylee meant the streets of Bakersfield. Monterey Street was a few blocks away from the circle, and Columbus was farther on, near the cemetery where his family lay.

As he drove around the circle a few times, he made note of the nearby businesses. There was a hospital a block away, and a few shops that had closed down. Nothing to make a light bulb go off in his head.

Monterey was much the same, although a lot of empty lots that used to have houses had tents and campers on them. He continued east, then north to Columbus. The street led him past several shopping centers that had closed down, and into another residential area. It dead-ended at Panorama Road on the bluffs, where the road to the county dump was gated-off from public access.

He laughed at that. Leave it to Kaylee to lead him on a wild goose chase to the dump.

Turning east on Panorama, he made random turns until he found himself at Hart Park. The large recreation area now resembled the campground at Buena Vista, with refugees living out of tents, campers and cars.

Idling the engine as he stared past the park into the mountains just beyond, JC was no closer to his answer. The itch to keep going still left him anxious, but he didn't have gas to waste when he didn't know where he was headed. The sky was beginning to brighten. As he glanced one last time at the shadow of the mountains, he saw a light fall behind the highest peak. Another meteor? No one had mentioned them in any of the discussions he'd overheard about the changes going on.

He put the car into gear and accelerated. Niki would freak when she woke up and her car was gone. If she'd even slept.

Was this their first fight? She probably thought so. He grinned when he thought about how often she'd snapped at him when they first got together. But a fight meant he argued back, and he didn't do that very often. Ever since he found his mom and sister under the front door of the apartment, nothing seemed worth fighting about. Nothing really mattered.

Having a fight meant they were in a relationship, at least where girls were concerned. He guessed by now that was what you'd call the way he and Niki were together. Even though they shared a tent with Antwon, they lived like a team. It was better than dating. They worked together for survival, which was much more important than trying to stay friends long enough to have a date to prom.

Shit. He had some kissing-up to do when he got back. Problem was, he still didn't know how to explain what was going on.

Chapter Twelve

The thin sunlight brightening the tent when Niki woke didn't pierce the shadows around her heart. She was alone. Antwon had come back last night, but if JC had, he hadn't wakened her. Dressing quickly, she hurried to fetch a bucket of hot water from the kitchen area, carrying it to the bathroom to wash up. Then she ate plain oatmeal with her coffee and wished she could get rid of the dread that filled her. She knew something was about to change.

Some of the other refugees at the lake were discussing the recent round of earthquakes. Niki had gotten to where she didn't notice the small ones any more than she would a passing train. News had come in about more cataclysms happening around the planet. Preachers were predicting the end of the world, and scientists were running out of plausible explanations for how the planet would go on in spite of it all.

She continually searched for sign of JC's return. She took her turn washing the cooking dishes in the washtubs, then wandered the lakeshore, unable to face the empty tent. She zipped her jacket up against the moist air seeping off the water and listened for the occasional pop in the water when a fish snagged an insect. A yellow Labrador Retriever ran up to her with a stick and dropped it at her feet. She tossed it down the shore and watched the dog run after it.

Normal.

New life and old life blending. One foot followed the other through each day, taking whatever came. The volcano hadn't caused any more problems, and neither had the latest quakes. Children laughed more and their parents snapped less often.

Normal.

She needed to make that a mantra, to remind her that everything was good. Because it sure didn't feel that way. It felt...unfinished. And it didn't help that JC had disappeared.

She circled around the lake to their tent and yanked the zipper open. The sight of JC sitting inside made her do a double-take to be sure she hadn't imagined him. He looked up but didn't speak. She stepped inside. "Hey."

"Hey."

Folding her sleeping bag and putting it away, she tried to figure out how to act. He probably expected pissed off, when all she wanted to do was hug him, she was so glad he'd come back. She couldn't care less that he had her car. She'd hated not knowing if she'd ever see him again.

The silence grated on her skin. She rubbed her palms over her arms.

"Cold?" JC asked.

"No." But she hugged herself when she sat as if she was freezing.

"I'm sorry."

She waited, but that was all he said. She grimaced.

What was he sorry for? Storming out? Wrecking her car? Being a guy? "It's okay, I guess."

He cleared his throat. "No. It's not. I was an asshat last night."

Niki bit her lip to keep from laughing. He really was an asshat. "It's okay."

JC jumped up and paced. "No, it isn't. I shouldn't treat you like that. I don't mean to, but I don't know how to explain it."

"Explain what? Isn't this where we were last night when you storm—when you left? I want to help but I'm afraid of pissing you off. Help me, JC."

He stopped pacing and set down that blasted beanie cap he always fidgeted with. His hair was tangled as if he'd slept in the cap, or pulled it on and off all night. He crossed to his chair and dragged it beside hers. "I'll try. But you're going to think I'm crazy."

Niki laughed. "I talk to dead people and *you're* crazy?"

"Yeah, well, you haven't heard me out." He leaned forward in his chair, resting his elbows on his knees. "Something is calling me to go east."

"You said something like that before. Is it Kaylee? Did you figure out what she was saying?"

"No. I spent the night driving around the streets she mentioned and there was nothing. No answers. Not even a clue."

She rested her hand on his wrist and his fidgeting stopped. "I'm sorry." She spoke softly, hoping to keep him calm. "So let's see what we can figure out together. Do you know anyone living east of us? Family?"

He laughed. "We're on the west coast. Everything is east of us."

"Good point. Okay. Who do you know who might

be important to see right now?"

"I don't know. I can't think of anyone. I never met any of my cousins or aunts and uncles in Oklahoma. But I don't think that's it."

"That's good. We narrowed it down a bit." Niki traced circles on the floor with the toe of her shoe while she thought. "Maybe the damage isn't so bad on the other side of the mountains, and we would have more normal lives there."

"You've listened to the radio reports. There isn't a state that hasn't been hit by something. That's why nobody came to save us. They're too busy saving themselves."

He was right. Which exhausted her not-so-vast store of ideas. "What do you think, then?"

"I think I'm going crazy."

"Well, you're taking me along for the ride, and this slow pace is killing me. Please fill me in before I go postal on you."

He sat up, adjusted his jeans and tossed his cap on the pile of sleeping bags. Then he ran his fingers through his hair. Just when she was ready to snap, he spoke. "Remember those asteroids?"

"Yeah. You guys said they could have caused whatever made the changes come."

"I don't think they're asteroids. What if…"

When he didn't continue she repeated, "What if…"

The silence was killing her. "JC, what else could they be? Bombs from Korea? Space junk finally falling to earth? Or do you think the entire universe is blowing up?" She clutched her thighs, her fingers pressing deep into her flesh. He was really scaring her.

"No. Crazier." He looked her in the eye. "What if they're people from another planet?"

She blew out all the breath she'd been holding. "Oh, you had me going there. I thought you were being serious."

He didn't smile, didn't look away.

"You. Aren't. Joking. Okay. Um. I've always thought aliens were only in the movies. Yeah, I know, I live in the movies. But I need your help here. Help me see how they could be real."

He took her hand, lowering his gaze. "I don't know how. It's just a feeling I have."

A ginormous ache filled her. He really believed, she could tell. And he needed her to believe. But there wasn't a switch she could flip to make herself think people really lived on other planets.

His voice came to her, barely above a whisper. "You think I'm crazy, too."

The pain in his words stabbed the shield her mind wanted to hold up. Niki fell to her knees in front of him. She placed her hands on either side of his face, lifting, forcing him to look at her. "JC, you are not crazy. I will never believe that you are. What I do believe is that I can trust you with my life. And I do."

"If I said we had to pack up everything right now and go, would you?"

"Yes."

"Even if I couldn't say where we were going?"

She laughed. "You haven't noticed I've been doing that from the start? You haven't steered me wrong yet."

Now he grinned. "You haven't gone without arguing."

She stuck her tongue out at him. "You didn't ask that. And I'm not promising to not…discuss the decision should the time come."

JC ruffled her hair. "That's my girl."

Niki rose up and pressed her lips against his. He sucked in a breath, then grabbed her shoulders and pulled her onto his lap. The camp chair wobbled but they didn't stop. He kissed her with a hunger that scared her as much as excited her. Her body needed the taste of him, the scent of him, the sound of his ragged breaths. She couldn't get close enough.

Suddenly the chair tipped and crashed over backwards. JC grunted when they hit the ground. Niki burst out laughing. "Are you okay?"

"I think I've developed a fear of kissing."

She laughed with him, and stole another taste of his lips.

The tent door unzipped and Antwon came in. "Aw, shit, you guys. I gotta sleep here, too." He turned to leave.

"Wait!" Niki climbed off JC and what was left of the chair. "We're not doing anything."

"That didn't look like nothing."

JC picked up the chair and tried to fit the pieces together. "We were only kissing. Then the chair broke."

"That must have been some kiss. I'm gonna go get me some dinner. Let me know when it's safe to come back."

JC followed him. "Wait, we'll come with you."

~*~

JC braced one arm on his shovel and wiped the sweat from his brow with the other. The sun was unbearably hot for March. The other guys on the line all wore ball caps, beanies like his, or bandana-type head wraps to keep off the sun. They dug without speaking, needing the energy for a day full of hard labor in the oil field. Grunts and the occasional spit were the only sounds they made. A CB radio inside one of the trucks parked nearby squawked occasionally but the static made it impossible to make out what was said.

Shoving his spade back into the rocky dirt, JC tossed another scoop of dirt onto the growing pile on the far side of the pipe. The pipelines were well marked, which made it pretty mindless work. Dig down and clear the dirt from around the pipe, then move to the end of the line and start again.

The periodic tremors went pretty much unnoticed anymore. Maybe girls who were silly enough to wear heels wobbled a bit more than usual when they walked, but to the guys he worked with, the little quakes weren't worth mentioning.

When the ground suddenly shook hard, then visibly bucked, everyone yelled. JC stumbled into the ditch, landing hard on his right arm. As he climbed back out, he heard an explosion followed by yells in the distance.

Antwon pointed at the black cloud rising. "Something ruptured. We'd better move."

Another explosion rang out, this one shaking the ground a little. The other guys were scrambling for their trucks. One of the older men called out, "Don't start the trucks! There could be gas leaking here. Just run."

Antwon glanced at JC before taking off after the others. JC followed. They stuck to the dirt road, but once they reached pavement they veered off in a direct line to the hills at the edge of the oilfields. Lungs burning, JC suddenly got a quick whiff of rotten eggs.

Hydrogen sulfide, the gas they were running from.

Ahead of him, a man collapsed. The other men continued to run, or broke off into another direction. JC ran toward the man. Antwon grabbed his arm. "No, man! Not without a mask!"

"But—"

"Move your ass!" One of the older men grabbed JC's hood and yanked, forcing him to follow.

Against his wishes, JC ran. And ran. And finally, when he couldn't breathe without pain, and the stitch in his side threatened to tear him in half, he cleared the rise of the hill. The men stumbled their way down, coming to a stop when they reached the highway at the foot of the hill.

JC bent and grasped his knees, trying to slow his breathing. His heart pounded in his ears. Antwon walked in slow circles around him as if to loosen his leg muscles after the run. Some of the men had dropped to sit on the ground and catch their breath.

When he thought he could speak, JC turned to Antwon. "Why didn't you let me help that guy? He's gonna die from the gas."

"Didn't you read the manual they gave you? You can't go into the gas without a mask or you'll die, too."

"But how can you just leave him?"

Antwon shook his head. "You have to. It's survival. You go for help. Radio for rescue, or whatever. But it's the only way to give him a chance. One of the guys with radios would've called it in. It's probably too late, though. If you'da gone in, that'd be one more rescuer risking his life to haul your sorry ass out."

JC felt like he was going to puke. He didn't know if it was the running or the frustration at not stopping to help the guy. Tugging at his beanie, he realized how lucky he was Antwon was there. The other men would have kept running, more than likely. "Thanks, man."

"No problem."

The sun had dropped partway behind the hills, casting a long shadow over the valley. JC gazed east, toward the lake. "Guess we might as well go home. The supervisor will fill out the report."

Nodding, Antwon started walking. "We'll have to leave early for work in the morning, since the dirt bike is still there."

Neither said a word until they reached the campground at the lake, when Antwon headed for the showers. JC had to see Niki first. She was serving stew in the kitchen. She smiled when she noticed him standing to one side, watching her.

"You're home early," she said.

He couldn't bring himself to smile back. Glancing at the other refugees waiting to eat, he simply said, "Accident in the field."

Her brows drew together but she didn't stop spooning stew into bowls. He wanted to hit the ladle from her hand and drag her to the tent. He wanted to throw what little stuff they had into their backpacks and get in her car and go. That itch inside him now had huge claws. It was time to leave before something bad happened.

Knowing all the disasters that had already hit, he wondered what could be next. As crazy as it all was, he wouldn't be surprised if a blizzard hit the valley floor. It had only snowed once in the south end of the Central Valley that he could remember, a couple of inches that stayed on the ground. But something crazy was going to happen and that's all his brain could come up with.

Rather than cause a scene, he waved at Niki and went to the tents. He detoured by way of Niki's car. He sat behind the wheel and messed with the wires until the engine jumped to life. One side of his mouth pulled back in a grin and he shook his head. He still got a kick out of knowing something he'd fixed worked right.

Popping open the hood, he looked for leaks and

checked the fluid level in the reservoir, then the engine and transmission oil levels. It all looked good. As he stood, he noticed a fiery arc streaming across the sky, larger than the ones he usually saw. He'd seen meteor showers that lasted a few days, but never for months. The whole universe must be falling apart.

Could that happen? Could all the stars be falling to pieces the way the earth seemed to be? The burning meteor disappeared behind Bear Mountain in the east without giving him an answer.

He scratched his head under his beanie. All the asteroids or meteors or whatever he'd been seeing fell in the same direction. He thought they normally sprinkled across the sky in different directions. In spite of what he'd said to Niki, he wasn't ready to think these burning objects were proof of intelligent life somewhere, but he had no other explanation. There were too many sightings to be coincidence.

In spite of some great movies, he refused to think their safety was threatened by an alien invasion. The people of earth were not a threat to anyone but themselves, so it didn't make sense someone would attack them. Maybe that confidence explained why he felt drawn to follow the meteors, rather than run the other way.

Antwon approached, rubbing a towel over his hair, which he now wore in cornrows. He stopped beside JC and looked at the engine. "Runnin' good?"

"Seems to be."

"Awesome."

"Yeah." JC shut it off. "I'm thinking we need to move on."

Chapter Thirteen

JC headed to the tent, turning on the lantern when they got inside.

Antwon tossed his towel aside. "Where we going this time?"

Picking up his backpack, JC propped it next to a chair so he could fill it. "I'm not sure. Bakersfield, to start."

Antwon nodded. "Okay." He reached for his own pack.

"You're not going to question me?"

He paused. "You haven't gotten me killed yet. Came close in the oilfield, but I caught you in time," he added with a cockeyed grin.

JC tucked his soap and toothbrush into a side pocket. When he knelt to roll up his sleeping bag, he heard Niki pull open the tent flaps.

"What are you doing?" She stood just inside, her hands on her hips.

"We need to leave here. Or go somewhere. I'm not sure which."

"So you were going to leave without telling me?"

His lips thinned. Why did girls always think like that? "No. I was packing while I waited for you to finish serving dinner."

She didn't move, didn't drop her hands from that pissed-off-mom position. She was going to make him explain it all again before she would pack her stuff, obviously. He sat back on his heels and met her glare.

"I thought we went over this last night and you were good with it."

"Yeah, but I didn't think it'd happen so soon. I hate doing anything without planning it out ahead of time."

He felt a wave of pity for her. They hadn't been able to plan anything since the twentieth of December. "Well, it's time to go. I don't think seeing that guy die in the oil fields had anything to do with it—"

"Somebody died?"

"Yeah. Just some guy. After the bigger tremors this afternoon. There were some gas leaks. But that's not why we're going."

"'We're going.' Just like that. I don't get a say in it?"

"You always have a say in what you do, Mouse. But I strongly suggest you come with us. I want you to."

She folded her arms across her chest. "Well, then, where are we going?"

"Let's plan on Bako to get some supplies. We need coolant for your car, just in case. And gas if we're going to get anywhere beyond that." He wasn't about to admit he hadn't thought that far ahead. He was running on gut instinct. And hoped it pointed the right direction.

"What about Lisa?"

He smiled. She was thinking beyond Bakersfield. "We'll go see her. Maybe we can convince her family to come, too. Let's play it by ear. Pack your stuff so we can get moving."

She moved quickly, stuffing her neatly folded clothes into her pack and gathering the little stuff. JC tied his rolled-up sleeping bag onto the backpack frame and folded the camp chairs. Antwon threw the flashlights and spare batteries into a box, along with the food they kept in the tent.

JC stood and spoke to Antwon. "Do we have some rope? You can put your bike in the trunk of the car. Save some gas. We'll have to tie the lid closed."

Grinning, Antwon picked up a partial box of packages of candy and headed toward the tent opening. "I'll see what I can find from our neighbors."

While he was gone, JC dismantled the tent and loaded the car. Antwon returned with a small piece of rope. Once the trunk was tied shut, the guys walked around to the doors. Niki had watched silently while the car was loaded, and now she looked around the lake at the other campsites.

"I should say good-bye. Tell Lillian she needs to schedule someone else in the kitchen." She didn't move.

"Okay, sure. We'll wait." He tried to figure out what was going on in her head when she still didn't go. "Would you rather stay here?"

She turned back and was chewing on her lip when she looked at him. "No. Not really."

"Is something else holding you back? Is Anne here?"

Niki glanced about. "No, I don't see her. I'll be right back." She jogged away.

Shaking his head, he ignored Antwon and bent to start the car. Out of habit, he scanned the radio stations but the dial didn't even hesitate at the places the stations used to come in. "It's crazy."

Antwon was stretched out in the back seat. "What is?"

"Why is everything still gone? No radio. No phones. It doesn't take this long to repair power lines or phone towers."

"I know. After a hurricane they get power back in a couple of weeks."

"It's like they're reinventing electricity. Even Oxy doesn't have power yet, and they have their own plant. It's creepy."

"No kidding. I wonder what is gonna happen. I mean, movies show stuff like this, but it never seems real."

"Well yeah," JC said with a laugh. "It usually has zombies. Or the damage happened ten years before the movie started. But we're here in the middle of it, minus zombies."

Joining the laughter, Antwon added, "Yeah, our movie is called The Zero Zombie Apocalypse."

"That's a dumb name, man."

"Well, what would you call a movie about the apocalypse without zombies?"

"The twentieth century." JC wondered if Antwon would get the joke, but his friend simply shrugged.

Niki came jogging back, her head down, and climbed behind the steering wheel. "Are we ready?"

"Yeah. Let's go."

They made their way slowly out of the campground and onto the empty highway. The lack of cars on the roads simply made it that much clearer recovery wasn't happening. Niki studied her dashboard and said, "We only have a quarter of a tank left."

Not good. By now all the stranded vehicles had likely been siphoned dry, and if the gas stations had anything left in their underground tanks, it was because no one could get it out. JC's gaze followed a coyote running just beyond their headlights. "I hope we can find some gas. Maybe we can get a hold of some bicycles, so we don't need gas."

"I had one at my uncle's house, but it's probably long gone by now," Antwon offered.

Niki was quiet until they closed in on the city limits. "Okay, where am I going?"

JC had no response. Whatever had told him it was time to move on wasn't providing directions. "I guess we should go to Lisa's house."

Her face, lit by dash lights, showed her astonishment. "So we really have no plan?"

He turned to look at the houses on the side of the road. Some had dim lights inside, but none shone with the brightness of electricity. He was surprised to realize that was what he expected to see. "Not yet. I'm playing it by ear."

"We're following your voices?"

Her sarcasm hurt. "No. I'm not hearing voices. It's kind of like when I checked on you at the apartments. I just knew I needed to."

That made her go quiet. At first he was glad, but then he felt guilty. When Niki got quiet, he had no idea what she was thinking. He liked it better when he had a clue. "I can't explain it. We need to do this. I don't know why. Can you trust me on that?"

She chewed her lip for the longest time. "Yeah. Guess I have to."

Antwon snorted in the back seat. JC rolled his eyes and leaned against the door. More meteors were falling, fading away quickly. He stared up at the stars. He'd always liked looking at the stars. He'd sneak out of the apartment as a kid when Mom was busy with Kaylee and sit on their tiny patio. For a few years, he'd wanted to be an astronaut, but that vanished when he got old enough to understand things like grades and scholarships. Some nights when he looked up there, he wished he could go home. Since he'd never lived anywhere but the apartment, he couldn't figure that one out. He'd finally decided he wanted a place to call his own.

While it didn't have the excitement of flying in space, he liked his job at the gym. People respected him for what he knew. No one treated him like a punk. Girls even flirted with him once in a while. Too bad he never could get up the nerve to do anything about it.

He missed working out. His daily run was okay, but it didn't give him the rush the weights did. The physical labor in the oilfields helped some. At least there he felt like he'd accomplished something by the end of the day. Maybe if they found a place to stay for a while he could help build homes. But he had a feeling they wouldn't be staying put anytime soon.

He shifted in his seat. The closer they got to Bako, the antsier he grew.

Niki sighed. "I miss my radio."

"Don't you have any cassettes?" He automatically reached over and punched the eject button on the radio. Nothing happened.

"Nah. They weren't in my budget. Lisa gave me an iPod for Christmas last year with a bunch of songs on it. It was in my apartment."

"Too bad we didn't go back there and try to dig out some of your stuff."

She shook her head. "I didn't want to see that place again. I still have nightmares about not getting out."

JC suddenly felt like he was going to puke, but it passed just as quickly as it hit. After that first day, the panic that he couldn't rescue her had passed. Thinking that way again made him sick. "We won't go back there."

He felt a sense of relief when Niki made the turn to take them to Lisa's house. A small *chink* of a piece falling into place. This was what they were supposed to be doing.

The front window was dimly lit. JC reached for his seatbelt. "Looks like they're home."

He and Antwon followed Niki up the path to the door. Even in the moonlight JC could tell the plywood siding hadn't been painted. That meant the government still hadn't come through with aid to help people get back on their feet. He didn't like that thought.

Lisa's husband, Paul, answered the door and pulled it open wide. "Come in, kids. We're playing board games."

JC hadn't met him before, and looked him over in the light from the kerosene lamp. Paul was an inch or so shorter than JC's six feet, and lean. His black, straight hair had lines of silver that picked up the light. He wore it in a ponytail. With his high cheekbones and hawk-like nose, JC guess Paul had some Native American blood in him.

Lisa, on the other hand, was shorter like Niki, with the roundness of a person who loved to cook and wanted to feed the world. Her pale blonde hair had grown out, leaving graying ash roots. She jumped up when she saw the group and pulled Antwon into her spot on the couch where she'd been playing a board game with her sons. "Here, play for me. I'm losing. You'll probably do better." She gave Niki a hug and smiled at JC, then offered them a drink.

JC shook his head. He hadn't figured out how to say what he needed to say. He was pretty sure they shouldn't talk in front of the kids. Looking first at Lisa, then at Paul, he asked, "Can we go sit in the other room?"

Lisa tipped her head, then smiled. "Sure. Come on."

When JC, Niki and Paul were seated at the kitchen table, Lisa set steaming coffee mugs in front of them and poured one for herself. Sitting, she glanced at her husband before speaking to JC. "Is everything okay?"

"Sort of." He unzipped his hoodie and shoved his hands into his pockets. "This is gonna sound weird, but I'll try and make sense. I think we need to leave the valley."

"Where will you go?" Lisa held his gaze.

"I'm not sure. I feel like we need to head over the mountains."

"Tehachapi? Mojave?" Paul asked. "Why there?"

"That's just it," JC answered. "I don't know."

Across the table, Niki rested her arms on the table and leaned forward. "Is it because of the gas leak at Elk Hills?"

"Not really." He tried to search his mind for where it started, and what he'd told Niki. Looking at her, keeping the others out of his focus, he began. "When I found Niki in her apartment, I felt like I was being pulled to that spot. It wasn't like, oh, I should go see if Niki is okay. I *had* to go find her, right then. This is the same thing. I'm being pulled to go over the mountains."

Now he glanced at the grown-ups to see their reactions. Surprisingly, they looked curious.

Paul swallowed some coffee and set his mug down. "Do you have family over that way? Either of you?"

Niki shook her head. JC said, "Not that I know of. Dad never talked about his people. But I don't think I'm supposed to find someone. I think we're supposed to stay there. Wherever."

"So you came to say good-bye?" Lisa asked Niki.

"I guess so. JC just said to come here first."

JC tugged at his beanie while gathering his courage. "I think we all need to go together."

Folding his arms across his chest, Paul sat back in his chair. "That's a pretty big step to take on a gut feeling."

Lisa placed her hand on Paul's shoulder. "His gut feelings saved Niki's life."

"But to leave everything. Pack up the cars and drag the kids into who knows what? We have no idea what conditions are like outside the valley. We have water here, food, and a place to trade for anything we might run short of. Can we risk giving up all that security?"

JC waited to see what Lisa would say. He wasn't sure Niki would go without them. And he didn't want to go without her.

But they had to. And he was pretty sure they needed to go soon.

Lisa asked Niki, "You're going with JC and Antwon even though you haven't located Crystal? Bakersfield is the place she'd come looking for you."

Niki closed her eyes and chewed her lip for the longest time. When she looked at JC, he relaxed. He could see her answer in her eyes, although hearing her ragged voice made his heart hurt. "Yeah. It won't be easy, but I trust him. He's already saved my butt a few times. And I have to accept that Crystal's probably dead."

Paul shook his head and wrapped his hands around his coffee mug. "I don't have your automatic reasons to trust JC. But I know you, Niki, and I know how much trust Lisa has in you. We've been storing supplies for years, waiting for a sign to bug out. I guess this is it. So it looks like we're going. We need to plan this out, though, JC. Let me get a pad of paper."

When he walked out of the room, Lisa placed

her hand on JC's. "I trust you, too. My husband will probably wish he'd said no at some point in the middle of this, but he'll go along with any reasonable decision. We have a trailer already stocked, but there is still a lot of work to do."

They made lists of what to pack and what was already stored in the two trailers. After the kids went to bed, JC, Antwon and Paul went to the garage. When Paul lifted the double-wide door and the lantern threw light on everything inside, JC just stared. W*hoa.*

The space looked like a mini big-box store. Metal shelves lined the walls and formed aisles through the back half. On the shelves were dried foods of every kind JC could imagine. Cans, too, restaurant-sized, filling the shelves. He followed Paul into the depths, saying, "Wow. Did you know something like this was going to happen? The big quake?"

"Not specifically. But even when I was in high school in the eighties, scientists were warning us of the probabilities. It's crazy not to plan. All around the world there are hurricanes and quakes each year, and lately tsunamis have been on the rise. No pun intended. We might be more technologically advanced than many countries, but we were stupid not to be more prepared."

"I guess you're right. How are we going to get all of this into the cars?"

Paul set the lantern on a workbench and folded his arms across his chest, looking about. "We're not. I had a contingent plan for a bug out, but I never considered it would be a long-term move. I should have bought a school bus."

Antwon asked, "What's a bug out?"

"It's what we're doing tonight. Pack up everything we can and go." Paul handed Antwon the notepad. "The pop-up camp trailer is stocked, so we'll just stuff as many more boxes as we can into the space between the built-in cabinets."

Leading the guys around the side of the garage, Paul pointed to a smaller, open trailer made from a pickup truck bed. "Then we load this one. I have netting, tarps and ropes, but I don't know how high we can really pile this thing without dumping the load while climbing up the mountain."

Antwon read off the first items on the list, and the men went to work. Paul lined up five large gas cans beside his SUV, to strap on once it was loaded. He carried out several tool boxes to be loaded last, so they'd be accessible. JC and Antwon filled their arms with food and tucked it into the pop-up trailer.

Paul rolled a metal drum out from behind the garage, lifted the hose from its holder and put the nozzle in Niki's gas tank. Manually operating the pump on the top, he filled her tank, then moved to the other two vehicles.

Inside the house, Niki and Lisa's oldest daughter, Destinee, packed food, clothes and blankets into the back of Lisa's small SUV under Lisa's supervision. Adrenaline kept Niki going long past when she would have normally gone to sleep.

She followed Paul, JC and Antwon into a large closet off the back bedroom. A locked gun case took up most of one wall of the closet. Crossbows and quivers hung on another. JC's eyes widened when Paul opened the safe and revealed all the handguns and rifles. The man could outfit a small army.

Paul tossed each of the guys a duffle bag. "Fill these. Niki, you grab some pillowcases and start loading ammo. We're not leaving any of this behind."

They did as he asked, wordlessly, and carried the bags out to Paul's full-size SUV. Niki thought about what lay ahead. She caught Lisa dumping a bucket of water behind the house and asked, "Do you think we're going to need all those guns?"

"There's no way of knowing what's ahead. I was surprised there wasn't more looting early on. The merchants were smart to dole out what they had rather than hoard it and tempt the low-lifes. But that avenue of supply is gone and nothing has come in to replace it. The farmer's markets won't be able to keep up. People are going to think they have no choice but to steal.

"The radio reports won't say why there are no trucks coming in from outside of the area. No helicopters bringing in relief supplies. Everyone seems to be in a stupor. Even after three months, and they're still waiting for help to come." Lisa put her arm across Niki's shoulders and led her toward the house. "I don't know what JC's 'seeing' or feeling, but I know something is going to come to a head soon. We plan to be ready to protect what's ours."

"Can you teach JC and Antwon how to shoot?"

"Yeah," Lisa said. "We can have daily practice once we get on the road. You need to learn, too. Destinee and the boys can shoot."

Lisa and Niki stood at the front door in the shadows of the lantern light spilling from inside. Antwon walked up from the garage just as JC and Paul came from the driveway. Paul crossed his arms and said, "I guess we should get some sleep. We can leave right after breakfast."

Chapter Fourteen

The drive up the mountain to Tehachapi passed much more quickly than JC expected. He'd never been on Highway 58 with so few cars headed in either direction. Antwon's dirt bike was strapped to the top of the small trailer, so he rode in the back seat of Niki's car next to a stack of Lisa's blankets and sheets. JC had large cans of fruit around his feet, since they didn't want to waste any space.

Their caravan had to pull off the freeway in Keene, where an overpass had collapsed. The back road into Tehachapi was blocked in several places from rockslides. All three vehicles, moving very slowly, made it safely over the off-road bypasses other drivers had created.

Patches of snow lay in northern-facing shadows, and the tops of the peaks were heavily painted in white. The air smelled of wood smoke, and JC guessed that was how everyone kept warm. At least in the mountains, most people had wood stoves for backup heat.

They stopped along the road in sight of houses on the edge of Tehachapi. Lisa took her two little boys off behind a pile of rocks. JC climbed out to let the cold air wake him up. The air was still, the quiet deafening. The lack of traffic sounds bugged him. So much about daily life these days bothered him, but when he couldn't hear other people moving around, he had a harder time fighting off the idea they were the last people alive.

Stupid thought. The lines at the refugee camps told him many people had survived. They either had nowhere to go, or no gas to get there, so it wasn't likely he'd find them on the road.

Paul met JC at Niki's car, where they checked the engine temperature. JC felt a bit of pride when he saw the car ran fine.

"Good job," Niki told him softly.

He scratched at his beanie. He hated when anyone said that, even though he loved it at the same time. "I'm glad it's working."

Paul dropped the hood and turned to JC. "Any idea where we should head?"

JC had been thinking about that on the ride. Almost as if he had some sort of meter inside, he could feel the pull of whatever called to him. The more they traveled, he expected to feel the distance was closing. Instead, it felt like whatever they were chasing kept moving, too. "I'm not sure. I don't think we've reached wherever we're supposed to be going. But we need to stop here, before we go on."

Paul lifted an eyebrow. "What for?"

JC shrugged and looked over the colorless valley. "Hopefully I'll know it when I find it."

"It wouldn't hurt if we could get a couple of large containers for water. We can fill them with snow. Or go north toward the Kern River and have plenty of water. I just don't want to do too much aimless driving and waste fuel." Paul wiped the back of his hand over his mouth, then walked away.

Antwon shoved his hands in his hoodie pockets. "He's right about fuel. His Explorer probably guzzles it."

"Yeah. I don't know how much is in those gas cans he has. I wish I knew where we are going. And how we're supposed to get there."

Lisa had given her kids some snacks and drink pouches, and it looked like they were ready to move on. While Destinee got them back into the car, the others discussed their destination.

Lisa said, "I think we should head toward the high school, or the park in town. They seem the most likely places to be the refugee centers."

"What kind of information do we need?" asked Niki.

All eyes turned on JC, making him squirm. "Let's do this logically. We need a place to camp, gas, and more water barrels. I guess we should do like Lisa says and see where we can find it."

They found the refugee center, but were told supplies were only available to locals. JC pressed his lips together. If that was going to be the answer everywhere they went, they wouldn't get far. Totally illogical, he knew, but he feared he'd brought everyone this far for nothing. He asked the man behind the desk if there was a place where they could camp.

"Well, most folks are staying in their own yards, if their homes aren't livable. But there's a place out in Sand Canyon that's letting people stay awhile." The worker gave them instructions on where to find the property. "I don't know if I'd go there myself, but in times like this, what can you do?"

That sounded ominous. But like the guy said, they didn't have a lot of choices. JC and Paul walked slowly back to the cars, where the women entertained the kids. JC watched some children playing at the playground as if it were just another day without school. He wished he had the luxury of innocence like that. But that world was gone. "Do you think we should go to Sand Canyon?"

Paul had his arms crossed over his chest. "I do. I knew a guy with some land up there. A lot of people homesteaded there, so they have wells, livestock, and some have solar or wind power. Probably some doomsday preppers up there, too, living off the grid. They might be functioning like before the quake."

Before the quake. JC was only nineteen and he could already talk about the good old days like an old grandpa. That wasn't a club he'd been looking forward to joining. "Sounds good. I wonder if they have hot showers."

"The girls would love that, wouldn't they?" Paul chuckled. "I guess we've made up our minds."

They explained their plans to Lisa and Niki, then once more loaded everyone into the cars. Niki let him drive, which surprised him. As she buckled her seatbelt, she explained. "I'm feeling kind of foggy today. I don't think I should be in charge of something like a car."

He and Antwon laughed. JC said, "You hardly ever drive any more. It's not surprising it feels strange."

"I know. Sometimes I wonder if I'd know how to turn on my laptop if I got it back."

Antwon grunted in agreement. "How long do you think it's gonna take them to get things back to normal?"

"I thought they'd have it fixed months ago," JC said. He followed Lisa's car, which followed Paul's. It seemed like they had sandwiched the kids between them to protect them. But he couldn't think of what they needed protecting from. Sometimes he thought enough people had died that there should be enough of everything left to go around. But that wouldn't last forever.

As they reached the outskirts of town, they passed a neighborhood that had burned to the ground. Gray, charred chimneys marked the foundations where much of the burned lumber remained.

Niki coughed. Then again, harder. JC picked up the bottled water on the seat between them and offered it to her. She waved it away, now coughing so hard she couldn't speak.

"Do you need me to pound your back? Should I pull over? Antwon, can you help her?" JC rattled off questions without waiting for responses. He swerved to the dirt shoulder and stepped on the emergency brake.

Niki gasped hard, clawing at her throat. JC jumped out of the car and ran to her door. Yanking it open, he unbuckled her belt. Her face glowed red. Tears streamed down her cheeks. Grabbing her shoulders, JC shook her.

"What is it? What can I do?"

She didn't answer. Her gasps grew softer.

JC's heart pounded in his chest. Niki's struggles grew weak. Her eyes rolled back in her head and she went limp.

"No!" JC pulled her out of the car and laid her on the ground.

Antwon knelt beside him and put two fingers to her throat. "Her pulse is good."

Pressing his ear close to Niki's nose, JC listened. She drew in a small breath. He closed his eyes and said a quick prayer of thanks.

Lisa and Paul came running from down the road where they'd stopped. Lisa's voice sounded frantic. "What happened?"

JC shook his head. "I don't know. She just started

coughing, then passed out."

"Is she breathing? Do we need to do the Heimlich?" Lisa loosened Niki's coat as she knelt opposite JC. As she did, Niki's eyelids fluttered.

"Wh—" Niki whispered.

"Are you okay?" JC lifted her head and released the breath he'd been holding.

"Why am I on the ground?" Niki struggled to sit, putting a hand to her forehead.

"You fainted. You were coughing."

She looked up at him and he could see when the memories came to her. "I was in a fire. Trapped. It happened when we passed those houses."

Lisa gently pushed the hair back from Niki's face. "You felt what someone else experienced, do you think? Has this been happening often?"

Niki frowned. "Just once, when we saw the first tidal wave. I drowned. Well, it felt like I drowned."

Continuing to run her fingers through Niki's hair, Lisa said, "Maybe it has to do with how you can see Anne and the other ghosts. And how JC gets those feelings about people and all."

"I guess." Niki stretched her arms. "Can I get up now? The ground is freezing."

Paul reached out a hand to her. "Now that we know you're okay, let's get back on the road. I'd like to be tucked in somewhere more defensible by nightfall."

JC forced himself to focus on the road, but he could still feel his heart pounding in his ears. He thought Niki was dying, and this time there was nothing he could do to save her. All his pain, all his fears, were too fresh to cope with the incident. Driving the car didn't burn off enough energy to calm him, and that energy made it hard to concentrate.

They took the freeway for a few miles and got off at Sand Canyon Road, heading north. They were on the desert side of the Sierra Nevada Mountains, so there were no trees and little brush. The hills had gone from golden brown on the west side of town to red, with white splashes of limestone. A wind farm dotted one hillside, and patches of sagebrush were splashed all around.

"Look, donkeys," Niki cried out. A sign near the driveway announced a donkey refuge, and a long line of pipe corrals housed the animals along the base of a hill.

Antwon leaned forward and propped his arms on the seat. "We should get a couple of them to pull the car."

"It would take a whole team, wouldn't it?" Niki asked.

"Probably." The wheels turned in JC's thoughts, and he was grateful for the distraction. If they had a wagon or cart, a donkey would be a big help. He wasn't sure how much feed, or what kind of feed they needed. But the pioneers had come clear across the country with livestock pulling wagons the size of a motor home. The idea needed more thought. He'd mention it to Paul when they stopped.

The houses here were spread out, all with outbuildings of assorted types in various states of repair. Some homes had boarded windows, or patchwork plywood repairs, but most looked livable. After a few more turns, Paul pulled to the side of the road at a fenced-off driveway. The adults got out of the cars and met him while Destinee sat with her brothers.

"This is the address the guy gave us." Paul shaded his eyes and looked up at the buildings.

Niki asked, "How do we get anyone to come out so we can ask about staying here?"

"I don't know. I guess I need to walk up there," Paul replied.

Lisa grabbed his arm. "Are you sure you should do that? What if he's some sort of crazy person?"

Niki agreed. "He could have a gun. Maybe you should take a gun with you."

Paul shook his head. "Then I'd look threatening and he'd be sure to shoot. Maybe I'll walk the fence line and see if I can find anyone outside. JC, Antwon, you boys go around that way."

"Sure." He and Antwon jogged back the way they'd come, turning at the end of the property and following the barbed-wire fence toward the hillside. A single home sat beneath a couple of small oak trees, and a dog lay by the back door.

JC stopped and whistled. The dog raised its head. He whistled again, and the dog saw him. JC called out, "Hello."

"Dude, why you talkin' to the dog?"

"I'm trying to get him to bark. Maybe his owner will come look."

"Oh, cool. Hey, dog. Come here, boy." Antwon waved his arms.

The dog put his head back down. JC grimaced. He picked up a small rock and tossed it a short distance from the dog, hoping to stir the animal. The dog didn't react. "Some watchdog," JC grumbled. "Let's see what's over the hill."

They climbed the small rise. As they neared the top, wind machines came into view on another hill. But what drew JC's attention was in the valley below.

At first glance, the land was untouched, the scrub brush and weeds scattered about. On closer inspection, he noticed circles of reddened cement, close to the color of the dirt in a grid pattern. Each circle had a darker square in its center.

Antwon came to a stop beside JC. "What do you think those are?"

"I saw something like that on TV. I'll bet there are underground bunkers all over the valley."

"No kidding? I'm not so sure I'd want to live underground."

JC nodded. "But if the alternative is death…"

"Good point."

The problem was trying to contact anyone inside the bunkers without looking like a threat. He wasn't anxious to look down the open end of a gun barrel. "Let's go see if Paul had better luck."

They found him waiting at the vehicles. He approached them when they drew near. "Did you find anyone?"

"No, but it looks like a whole neighborhood has moved in underground in the next valley. If these people are doomsday preppers, we might not want to try to contact them."

"Yeah, no kidding. I wonder if anyone actually lives in the house up front here, or if it's just a decoy."

JC leaned against Niki's car. "There's a dog on the back steps of the house, but we couldn't get him to bark."

"Odd," Paul said. "You'd think they'd have watchdogs."

"And cameras. The people on TV have infrared cameras, motion sensors, the whole deal."

"I'm not liking this." Paul scanned the hillside, then looked both ways on the road. "I think we need to put some space between us and the preppers. We'll set up camp farther up the valley, if we can find a spot."

As they broke up to return to their respective cars, a

four-wheel ATC came down the driveway and stopped at the gate. A short, older man with a rifle under his arm stepped off the cycle and walked toward them, remaining inside the gate. "What can I do for you folks?"

Paul motioned to JC as he went around his Explorer to talk to the man. JC moved casually and picked up the hand gun Paul had told him to keep under his seat. He pocketed it and stayed by Niki's car.

Paul smiled at the stranger. "Hi. I'm Paul Green, and these are my friends and family. We left Bakersfield this morning and we need a place to camp. Someone in Tehachapi suggested your place. We have our own supplies. We just want a safe place to park."

The man eyed them and the two trailers. He didn't introduce himself, JC noticed. He kept his rifle pointed skyward. The old guy said, "I don't have hook ups or anything. You were misled."

Paul pushed the issue. "We don't need electricity. We even have water, although if there is a place around here, a creek or something, we'd appreciate being able to top off our barrel."

The old man pointed toward the northwest with his rifle. "If you head back to Caliente, you can camp at Lake Isabella. Or fill up at the Kern River anywhere in there. Just keep the kids back from the river. The current is stronger than it looks."

JC shook his head. No one would be wading in the water when there was snow on the ground. He appreciated the guy's intention, but wondered if the guy thought they were idiots.

Paul held out his right hand to shake, but the guy ignored it. Paul said, "I appreciate the information. We'll get out of your hair."

Without speaking to their group, Paul got back in

his Explorer and started it up. Lisa and JC pulled out to follow him up the road.

Chapter Fifteen

Paul drove into a small clearing and waved for the others to form a small circle. Niki let out a sigh and realized she'd been holding her breath since they stopped at the prepper's property. That place gave her a bad feeling, and she'd been relieved when they drove away. She guessed the time to be mid-afternoon.

Paul wanted to have camp set up before dark. He explained while they unloaded the pop-up trailer. "We have no idea what to expect here, outside city limits. We don't know if these people are living off the land, or if they've been able to get to town for supplies. Hopefully most of them laid in emergency rations ahead of time, but we need to assume we'll come across some who haven't."

While Lisa, Destinee and Niki planned what to cook for dinner, the guys went hunting. They took their crossbows and knives, not wanting to draw attention to their camp with gunfire.

Lisa took advantage of the absence of men to pry. "So, you and JC are really doing well?"

"We're surviving, like everyone else." She measured

a small amount of water to rehydrate some onions.

"I mean as a couple. I said before I could see how much he loves you. When you passed out in Tehachapi, he looked like his life was ending."

Really? All at once, Niki felt sad for him but happy for them. "That poor guy. He's been through so much because of me."

"Exactly. If he didn't have you to focus on, his grief might have led him to give up his struggles to survive."

Niki slid onto the padded bench seat at the table, remembering the old days when she, Anne and Lisa would gossip. She wasn't surprised to see her friend sitting opposite her. "Anne is here. She wants to know where her cup is."

Lisa sniffled.

"Are you okay?"

Wiping her nose with a handkerchief, Lisa then washed her hands before sitting. She took a sip of her tea, and said. "I miss Anne. I miss everyone we worked with, but they're all still alive, of course. I feel guilty about Anne. I assigned her to that shift. It's my fault she was there when the quake hit."

"How do you think I feel," Niki argued. "That was my position she took over. I should have been there, not her."

Anne waved her arms and shook her head. "It happened the way it was supposed to. No one is to blame. You guys can't carry this burden with you."

Niki nodded, swallowing the ache growing in her throat. "Anne says for us to knock it off. It's nobody's fault. But I still miss her."

"Me, too. Let's get back to happy times. You never told me how you and JC met. How he even knew where to look for you."

Niki wrinkled her nose and turned to lean her back against the wall of the trailer, her feet sticking into the aisle. "Oh, that. It's kind of embarrassing. I didn't even know his name, but he remembered me from school. One of his friends started calling me Mouse, and they teased me all year long."

Lisa smiled. "Well, that's kind of cute. Maybe."

"No, it wasn't. Or I didn't think so. JC did, though, and he still slips and calls me that sometimes."

"A pet name. So sweet."

Niki sipped her drink. "Whatever. He admits he had a crush on me but didn't have the guts to ask me out."

"Well, some boys just need a little nudge."

"Is that what they call it? The San Andreas Nudge?" She laughed, as did Anne and Lisa. "He is so different than I thought he was. And I was such a bitch to him! I don't know how I will ever make it up to him."

"He doesn't seem affected by it, if you really were mean."

Niki wrinkled her nose. "I was so bad. It was like I was still in high school."

"You mean, you lashed out and asked questions later?"

"Pretty much." Niki shook her head and sipped her tea. "One minute I'd snap his head off, the next, cling to him like I was drowning."

"And how did he react."

Thinking about it made her throat burn. "He just took it. I don't know if he was in shock the first few weeks, since he saw his mom and sister dead, or if he thought he deserved to be treated badly. That scares me the most, if he thought it was okay for me to treat him that way."

"Well, you are nice to him now, aren't you?"

Niki nodded. "I'm learning to be. I don't know why it's so hard to do. He's so good to me."

"I'm gonna be nosy..." Lisa said.

"When are you not?"

"Who said I love you first?"

Niki frowned. "I don't think either of us has said it. It's not like we're dating and we can make out in the car after a movie. And Antwon sleeps in the same tent."

"Maybe Paul and I can plan a distraction for Antwon one night. He was really good playing games with the boys."

"Oh, God, no, please. How awkward would that be? *Ewww.*"

"This is a weird time to be falling in love. I don't envy you. I'm sure once things become more like before and we all have real homes, you two will find you have a strong foundation to a great romance."

Niki bit back the *whatever* that wanted to escape her lips. As weird as it felt to think she might be falling in love, it was even weirder to think about spending the rest of her life with someone. Even JC.

"You two would have such cute kids, with his curls and your beautiful gray eyes."

Niki stared at Lisa. "You can think about bringing kids into this madness?"

Lisa smiled gently. "Maybe since I have kids, I can't imagine not having them. Kids are adaptable. Yours wouldn't know that things had ever been any different. The world will go on. We need to keep it populated."

Looking down at her mug, Niki said, "You have a better outlook than I do."

Kids. She couldn't imagine being a mother, even in the world before the quake. No matter how much she cared for JC, she didn't see that changing. She needed to do everything she could to make sure she never slept with him, to be safe.

~*~

Paul tossed a pebble into a stand of brush, but nothing scampered out. He walked on. "You say they have bunkers in the next valley? I had a chance to buy some old shipping containers in the nineties, but let it pass. I considered buying some acreage near Glenville and sinking them in the ground for a bomb shelter. That was when we all thought the end of days would come from nuclear weapons."

Antwon lifted his crossbow and swung in an arc as if scouting the area. "What do you think happened to all those weapons? If they had quakes and hurricanes in Korea like we had here, how did they keep those from detonating? Or leaking?"

"That's a good question," Paul answered. "We can hope they were adequately housed so if there was any sort of leak, it was adequately contained. I hate to think of those poor people suffering radiation sickness on top of what we've been through."

Antwon grinned. "You sound like a teacher."

"A professor, actually."

JC looked back at the older man. "What did you teach?"

"American history. Some Native American studies."

"Were your ancestors Indians?"

"I'm Hopi. Three-quarters Hopi, one-quarter Mexican. We didn't live near the pueblos, and my folks didn't follow any of the traditions, but my granny did. Enough that I wanted to know more when I got to college."

JC held up a hand to block the setting sun and

looked for paths on the hills that meant animals traveled there regularly. "That's pretty cool you know where your ancestors came from."

Paul glanced at him in surprise. "You don't know who yours are? Where they immigrated from?"

"Nah. Mom's folks were from Oklahoma. For all I know, Dad sprang from a patch of weeds in Taft."

"Ah. Not a candidate for Father of the Year, I take it."

JC laughed. "That's a good way to put it." He liked Paul. The guy talked straight with him, didn't judge. JC already trusted his judgment, which he knew would make life a lot easier with everything around them so crazy. The weight of decision-making had JC worn out. Keeping Niki safe, making sure they had food, transportation, and shelter. Antwon probably had opinions, but he kept them to himself.

Niki certainly had opinions, and she kept nothing to herself. JC smiled. She was nothing like the Mouse who lived in his head the year before the quake. He liked the real girl so much more.

A shot rang out to the west. Paul held up a hand for silence.

JC listened, but couldn't hear a thing. He motioned to get Paul's attention and pointed back the way they'd come. Paul nodded.

Turning around, JC led the way with Antwon close behind. Paul took the rear, walking backwards to keep watch. They moved with stealth, knowing there was nowhere to hide should anyone come upon them. JC placed his feet as carefully as he could to avoid kicking a rock or breaking a twig.

He scanned the hills again, as if a cave or group of trees would magically appear. Acid burned in his stomach. They were sitting ducks if someone was after them. But no one knew they were there.

JC heard a bullet whiz by, then heard the gun fire. Paul yelled and crumpled to the ground. Antwon spun, pointing his crossbow as he looked for the shooter. JC searched the hillside above them, but saw no one.

He hurried to Paul's side. "Are you okay?"

Paul clutched his outer thigh, where blood colored his jeans. "I'm hit. I don't know if I can walk back to the cars. But we can't stay here."

"Let me help you up." JC bent under Paul's arm on his injured side while Antwon pulled his other arm.

When he was standing, Paul tested his leg. "Damn. No, I can't walk. Can you think of anything back at the camp I can use as a crutch?"

JC couldn't. "Just lean on me."

Paul did, and they hobbled a short distance before he begged them to stop.

Antwon came around to Paul's other side and held his crossbow out to JC. "Hold this. Let me try something."

JC dropped Paul's arm and took the weapon, moving aside. "What are you gonna do?"

"Remember at the lake? The trailer that fell on the kid?"

As JC nodded, Antwon bent, put one arm behind Paul's knees and the other around his shoulders. "Hold on." He straightened, lifting Paul.

"Put me down, you'll hurt yourself," Paul yelled.

"It's okay," JC said. "I think he has you."

Antwon walked stiffly down the path with Paul in his arms. JC followed, amazed. They made it back to camp. The women rushed out of the pop-up trailer.

"What happened?" Lisa called.

"What's he doing?" asked Niki.

Paul hobbled toward the trailer. "It's not as bad as it looks, but it hurts. We need to clean it up."

Lisa told her daughter to get the first aid kit from the SUV as she helped Paul into the trailer. Destinee rushed to do so.

Niki stopped in front of JC. "How did he do that?"

"He got shot—"

"No," she interrupted. "How did Antwon carry Paul? He's a scrawny dude."

JC looked at his friend for permission, and Antwon nodded. "It was the same as he did with the trailer. He's got strength when it needs it. It's weird, isn't it?"

Niki studied Antwon for a moment, then offered him a cockeyed smile. "I guess that makes him one of us."

Antwon grinned. "Yep. I'm a crazy mo-fo, too."

~*~

Niki handed one of two mugs of hot cocoa to Destinee, then sat next to JC at the campfire. Lisa had questioned the advisability of a fire, if someone had tried to kill them, but Paul said if the shooter had been aiming for them, he would have kept shooting.

"It was a stray bullet from a lousy hunter. I'm sure of it. I don't think we're under threat here. Just to be safe, we'll move on in the morning," Paul finished.

"Where will we go?" Destinee asked.

Paul looked at JC. "I'm interested to hear your opinion on this. I was listening to chatter on the radio on the ride up the mountain. Seems a lot of people are headed out to some lake outside California City."

Lisa frowned. "I don't remember a lake outside California City."

"It didn't used to be there." Paul scratched at the

bandages on his thigh. "Well, it was a dry lake. But the changes brought up water. Everyone has a different reason for going there, but there are enough of them doing so, I think it's worth checking out."

JC nodded. "Sounds good."

Niki listened to their discussion, when her vision grew hazy. She recognized the blackout that came with her visions of death. Her heart raced and she broke out in sweat. A pale cliff appeared in front of her. Walking in the shadows below, she looked up at a shell-shaped opening in the cliff wall. Dwellings lined the small cave, small adobe buildings with open windows and wooden doors.

After climbing a ladder of footholds carved into the rocky face, she stood in the mouth of the cave and looked outward over the red desert.

"Niki?" JC's voice called her back to the campsite.

Blinking, Niki tried to shake the vision. "What?"

He leaned close and spoke into her ear. "Your hands were shaking like crazy. I'm surprised that cocoa didn't burn your hand when it splashed you."

Her right hand was wet. Wiping it on her jeans, she whispered back, "I had another one of those visions."

"Where someone died?"

"No. I don't know. I was in a cave—"

"Everything okay?" Lisa interrupted.

Feeling like she'd been caught passing notes in class, Niki looked away. "Fine."

"You looked a little, well, distant, while staring into the fire. I was worried…"

"I said I'm fine. Really. I'm not a freak. You guys don't have to keep watching me." It felt like everyone was staring at her. Snapping like a bitch probably didn't help. But she wished she could just be normal. Be left alone.

"We're concerned because we love you, Niki," Lisa said softly. "It's okay to tell us if you're having visions."

How did she know? Niki took a quick gulp of her cocoa and regretted it when it burned the roof of her mouth.

Paul set his mug in the dirt. "I would be very grateful to hear what you see, if you think it might affect us. If it's some kind of warning."

"How could they be warnings? I'm pretty sure those other people died."

"I wasn't sure what you saw." Paul smiled and looked at his kids. "Maybe I'm just hoping someone will tell us where we are going."

She considered how the cave might tie in with where they were headed, but without knowing where it was, she couldn't suggest they go there. "I don't think this vision was a sign. I don't know where I was, and I didn't see any people."

"What did you see?" JC asked.

"There was a cave in a cliff, like, halfway up. It had houses inside, like the Native American pueblos. I climbed up into it."

Paul smiled. "Like Canyon de Chelly? In Arizona?"

"I don't know what that is."

"I like to think it's where my ancestors came from. The Anasazi, or Ancient Ones, who descended into the Pueblo tribes. I visited some of the cave dwellings when I was in college."

Lisa turned to her husband. "Do you think we're supposed to go there?"

Shaking his head, Paul said, "I can't think why. It's assumed the Anasazi left when they'd used up the resources. We wouldn't be any better off there than here. Possibly worse, if there's no water."

Niki sighed. For a moment she thought there was meaning in her visions, but it looked like they were just random events.

~*~

They bugged out the next morning, driving back to Highway 58 and heading east into the Mojave Desert. Only three other cars travelled in their direction, but once they merged onto the 14, two more cars joined them from the south.

Niki watched the cars in her rearview mirror. "I haven't seen this much traffic since the day of the earthquake."

"Maybe it means things are better on this side of the mountains," Antwon said.

After glancing at JC's expression, Niki didn't think so. "Maybe we're just headed the right way, for a change."

JC nodded. "We're getting closer."

"Closer to what? Where?"

He stared off into the flat horizon. "Wish I knew."

As they passed through California City, the number of cars on the road grew to ten or twelve. Niki felt uneasy. "Where are they going?"

"Paul said people were talking about the lake out here. Word gets around."

She pressed a hand to her stomach, but the butterflies didn't calm. "I have a funny feeling about this."

JC shifted to study her. "Funny good or funny bad?"

"Wish I knew."

He shook his head with a smile.

Half an hour later, Paul slowed to turn onto a dirt road, following the two cars in front of him. Lisa and Niki turned, too. As Niki watched in her mirror, the vehicles behind followed. She focused on the road ahead, keeping some distance between Lisa's car and hers to keep from getting lost in the dust. "This seems to be a popular place."

"Wonder what's here?" Antwon muttered.

They cleared a small rise and saw tents in the distance. JC grunted. "Looks like a circus."

Large white canvas structures clustered to one side of the gathering, and family-sized tents of all colors were sprinkled between motor homes, fifth wheels and pop-up trailers. As they drew near, Niki wondered what drew all these people to one spot.

Paul pulled out of line and gave the signal to "circle the wagons." Lisa and Niki turned and parked in a line with another row of campers. Niki stepped out of the car and coughed at the white dust surrounding them. She walked around the cars to talk to Lisa. "What do you think?"

Lisa blocked the sun from her eyes with her hand. "I'm not sure yet. What do you say?"

Zipping her jacket, Niki replied, "I say it's crazy. Twice as many people as were at Buena Vista."

JC approached. "That's a lot of people, seeing as this isn't a campground. No bathrooms or running water. No fish in the lake. No logical reason to leave the city."

"Well," Lisa added thoughtfully, "if their homes were destroyed and they didn't own the property, they had no reason to stay put."

"True," JC replied.

Paul thumped his hand on the pop up trailer. "Let's set up camp."

With a small grin, Lisa whispered to Niki, "I guess he's not having any second thoughts about coming here." She turned back to her husband. "You need to get off that leg. We'll set up camp. You go rest."

Chapter Sixteen

As the sun sank lower in the sky, the air grew colder. JC and Antwon had walked about a mile from the lake in search of firewood. They had enough for one night, but JC wanted more. But not badly enough to get lost in the dark. "Let's go back."

They hadn't gone far when drumbeats reached JC's ears. A few minutes later, wailing singers joined in. "I wonder what that is."

"Sounds like a sing-a-long."

"It's not any song I've heard before."

When they reached their own campsite, JC set the wood near the storage trailer. Lisa's sons ran to them. "They're having a pow-wow. Come see." Without waiting, they ran off the way they'd come.

The singing grew louder. He and Antwon followed the path the boys took between campsites to the far side of the large tents. Native American men sat in a small circle chanting and playing their drums in a traditional song. Others, wearing feathered and colorful costumes, danced in a circle. Women in long skirts, their black hair braided, shuffled around the outside of the ring of dancers.

JC searched the gathered crowd for Niki and the others. She waved a hand and he made his way to her. Paul stood behind Lisa and the girls, leaning on a crutch he had borrowed from somewhere. He nodded when JC walked up.

"I was afraid you guys would miss this," Paul said, leaning close and speaking softly.

"What is it? I mean, I know it's a pow-wow, but…"

"They're celebrating the Earth Mother. You can tell by their dress they aren't all from the same tribe. I'm not even sure what language they're singing in." Paul motioned toward a few gray-haired men who sat in chairs near a fire. "I asked the elders and they explained what they were doing."

"Oh." JC noticed some young boys imitating the moves of the older ones. Some wore jeans, some, buckskin-looking pants with fringe down the legs. He couldn't explain the envy that suddenly burned fiery in his gut. Those little kids knew more about their people, a group dying out by assimilation, than he did about his family. Whether his mom didn't care enough to tell him her stories, or if she just didn't know them, they were lost with her.

He had nothing to tell his kids someday about family traditions. The envy turned to sadness. He had nothing, in more ways than one.

Kaylee began to chant in his head, matching the sounds of the singers. He couldn't make out her words, either. Then she laughed and was silent.

Paul knelt down and spoke to his kids. Niki rolled to her feet and tucked her arm through JC's, leaning on him slightly. "Isn't it beautiful?"

"Yeah, it's cool." The drums were hypnotic, as if his

pulse beat in the same rhythm. The singing pulled him in, too. It was more like a wail, lots of vowels and no hard consonants. The longer he listened, he could tell when it repeated. "They just sing the same thing over and over?"

Niki lifted one shoulder. "Dunno. Sounds like it."

The song went on. The sky was dark now, the fire in the center of the dance circle lit everyone with a warm, golden glow. Niki rested her head on JC's shoulder and he felt more relaxed than he could remember.

Tipping his head back, he scanned the sky for familiar constellations. One bright star caught his attention, although he couldn't name it. There shouldn't be a bright star in that spot. He realized it was getting bigger. It moved slowly, then its arc changed and it began to fall.

The meteor was amazing to watch, beautiful and fierce with a white trail glowing behind it. As it grew brighter, others noticed, pointing at the sky.

It continued to get larger. JC tensed. It was coming their way. He tugged his arm free of Niki and pulled her tightly to his side.

"What?" She glanced up. "Oh my God, what is it?"

"Meteor. It's too big. It's going to hit nearby."

"It's going to hit us?"

Paul and Lisa stood. Paul said, "It will probably burn up in the atmosphere. They usually do."

As soon as he said that, the meteor exploded, burning as bright as the sun. People around them cried out, covering their eyes. An explosion rang like a sonic boom. A wave of hot air blasted them, toppling tents and the people in the crowd.

JC rolled as he fell to protect Niki. Antwon landed across their legs. Lisa's boys were crying, as were most of the children at the bonfire.

The ground shook, and thunder boomed again. A woman nearby screamed and begged Jesus to save them.

After Antwon got up, JC scooted off Niki. "You okay?"

"Everyone okay?" Paul echoed.

They climbed to their feet, dusting themselves off. Niki held onto JC's arm. "What was that?"

"Meteor, I guess," JC answered.

"Meteorite, you mean." Paul combed his fingers through Destinee's hair where she stood with her arms wrapped around him. "Once it landed, it became a meteorite."

"Are we gonna die?" asked the youngest boy.

"Not tonight, hon." Lisa gave him a pat on the head.

"Not from that meteorite. But I think now would be a good time to go to bed. Mom will read you some stories." Paul held JC back when Lisa led their kids away. He spoke softly. "That was too close for comfort."

"How close do you think it hit?" Niki asked. They walked slowly back to their campsite.

"It could be fifty miles away, or more. But if life was a game of horseshoes, that's 'closies.'"

JC understood immediately. They were the peg the horseshoe had been tossed at, and it landed just off course.

Antwon caught up to walk next to Paul. "Do you think all these quakes have been caused by asteroids? Or meteorites? Are they going to keep falling?"

"No, I don't think that's the case, from what I've gathered over the radio. It's like the earth has the flu and pneumonia, and just got bitten by a mosquito. Let's hope that mosquito wasn't carrying malaria."

~*~

The next morning, JC told Paul he was going to look for more firewood and he took off on the dirt bike in the direction of the meteorite impact. Unsure why, he had to see for himself where it landed. Not that he thought it was too close for comfort, or he thought the next one might kill them. He'd been certain the asteroids he'd seen the past few months led him to this area, since they all seemed to point this way. He just had to see for himself what he'd been following.

Maybe seeing would lead him to the reason why.

Circling to the north of a rocky mound, JC tried to gauge where the thing would have landed. He expected a crater the size of Kern County, miles and miles across, judging from the size of fireball they'd witnessed and the way the ground had shaken.

What he found was disappointing—a pit closer to the size of a swimming pool dug into the barren flatlands. It wasn't much deeper than a pool, either. Walking around the edge, he searched the hole for a sign of the rock that had caused it. It must have buried itself, because he saw only dirt.

He scanned the land nearby, checking out anything that looked out of place, and found half a dozen smaller pits scattered in the area. He guessed when the meteor exploded in the atmosphere, all the smaller pieces rained down.

When he got back to camp, he searched out Paul.

Paul glanced at the empty milk crate on the back of the dirt bike. "No luck?"

"Huh?" JC looked at the crate and remembered he was supposed to have hunted for firewood. "I, uh, forgot. I got distracted. I thought you might want to see it, too."

"See what?"

"The crater. Where the thing landed last night." In his excitement, JC waved his arms around while describing what he saw. "There are actually a bunch of little ones and one bigger one. But not as big as I expected."

"We're lucky it exploded. That blast of air we felt might have been a lot hotter if it hadn't. Let's go get the Explorer and you can show me where it hit."

~*~

Niki dried the last pan and put it in the cupboard, then followed Destinee to the bonfire where the others already were. The crowd surrounding the singers and dancers was twice as large as the night before. Someone had set up a table with fry bread, the light, cinnamon coated treat, and fruit punch, for everyone to enjoy. The girls each took a piece of bread, although Niki passed on the drink.

As she nibbled, she walked around the circle looking for JC. And did a double-take when she saw his mom and Kaylee standing next to him. He looked so much like his mom, but had lighter coloring. They nodded in time to the drum beat as though his mom was still alive and enjoying the pow-wow.

He smiled when he noticed her. She waved and picked up her pace. JC moved aside so Niki could stand between him and Lisa. He tore off a piece of Niki's fry bread and popped it in his mouth.

"Hey," Niki complained playfully. "Get your own."

She continued to watch him, trying to decide whether to tell him about his family. Finally deciding he deserved to know, she drew in a deep breath. "Your mom and Kaylee are here."

His eyes found hers, but he didn't turn his head. "They are?"

She nodded. "Kaylee is sitting with the boys, and your mom is standing next to me. She's really enjoying herself."

He dropped his head. "That's good."

Niki felt bad, thinking she made him sad. Slipping her arm around his, she hugged it to her. "I'm glad you're here with me."

Staring into the firelight, he said, "Me, too."

The singers sang into the night. The younger dancers grew tired and sat with the elders, but the others kept circling. Niki leaned forward to talk to Paul, who stood on the other side of JC. "Why do they keep going? Don't they get tired?"

"Sure they do, but the song and dances are like a prayer. They want to keep the vigil going, so the Old Ones Who Walk with the Stars will smile on us and bless us by returning the earth to us."

"What do you mean? Are the gods taking the earth away from us? Punishing us with death, or something?"

He crossed behind JC and stood on Niki's other side. "No. At least, not as I understand it. We've brought it on ourselves by disrespecting the Earth Mother. Now we must ask for forgiveness."

A bit of understanding sank in. She smiled. "It's a prayer circle."

"Pretty much."

"So, if we aren't singing along, we should be praying."

"Couldn't hurt." Paul grinned at her and went back to Lisa.

Niki wasn't used to praying, not in a formal sense. She probably begged, *please let this happen*, twenty times a day, but she doubted that counted. Most of her foster parents had gone to church every Sunday, so she knew the Our Father and Apostle's Creed, but doubted those fit, either. Closing her eyes, she decided to wing it.

Dear God, please let the earth heal. We've screwed it up pretty badly, I know, but we're trying to learn to fix it. Please give us a chance to get it right.

She opened her eyes again, then remembered to add, *Amen.*

Feeling more a part of the activities now, she squeezed JC's arm again. He smiled, but kept watching the dance.

A murmur began at the far end of the audience, and the crowd divided. Niki rose on her toes to see. "What's happening?"

JC barely looked in that direction. "Some more dancers are here, that's all."

Peering between the heads of those who stood in her way, Niki was able to make out fifteen or twenty young men and women joining in the crowd. She didn't understand why everyone was whispering about them. They all wore white, and their clothing looked like traditional costumes. Bright reds and turquoise on the breechcloths or aprons some men had on, and turquoise moccasin boots. Nothing separated them from the others who'd been there all evening.

Losing interest, Niki turned back to the dancers. The newcomers joined the dance, performing their own steps. The audience went back to whatever they'd been doing before the arrival of the new group.

An hour or so after Lisa took the boys back to the campsite, Niki rested her head on JC's shoulder. The crowd was thinning, the full moon on the ascent.

"Tired?" JC asked.

"Kind of. But I don't know why. It's not like I do anything these days."

"You do your share. You want to go back?"

She shook her head. "I like watching this. I miss TV and movies."

"You could always watch Lisa's DVDs with her kids."

"I think you and Antwon would enjoy those more than I do. I'd love to have a book to read, though."

JC slipped his arm around her back. "I bet if you ask around, someone has books they'd loan you. No one seems to be in any hurry to leave."

"That's so weird. Why are we here? What's so special about this place? There must be a thousand people here by now." What really made her curious was the difference in how they'd arrived there, versus landing at Lake Buena Vista. Everyone at Buena Vista seemed to have stopped at the first available campground.

But here, in the middle of nowhere, people gathered as though the event had been planned long in advance. She would never claim to understand what motivated people, so trying to figure this out was a wasted effort.

The drummers and singers stopped with a suddenness that left Niki hanging. The crowd waited in silence. One of the elders stood. "That's all for tonight. We will gather again tomorrow."

The audience sighed almost as one and wandered off in small groups. Niki watched the drummers pack up their drums. The bonfire had burned low and a man with a shovel put it out. Someone lit a lantern at the fry bread table.

JC gave Niki a one-armed hug. "Ready?"

"Not yet." The energy of that spot was so calming, she hated to leave.

The latecomers, the natives dressed in white, approached the two elder men who remained near the drum circle. A young man about Niki's age seemed to be the head of their group. He spoke to the old man in a language Niki didn't recognize.

The old man tipped his head to one side and seemed to struggle with his words in reply.

The young man looked back at his friends and spoke again to the old man.

Niki moved closer, drawn to the young guy. The movement of his hands didn't make the strange language any clearer. Niki's vision darkened around the edges, but she didn't black out. She saw herself in a hole in the ground, at the foot of a ladder leading out.

Anne appeared on the other side of the natives. "He's explaining how he got here."

Niki repeated what Anne said and the old man looked at her, startled. "You understand him? What does he say?"

JC and Paul stood behind her. Paul touched Niki's shoulder. "You speak his language?"

"No," she said. "But I see what he sees, I think. Anne told me what he's saying."

"Describe it," Paul said.

As she did, Niki found herself using the same motions as the young guy. "There was a big flash in the sky and a hole opened up. They used a ladder to climb out of the hole, leaving their land and finding themselves in the desert. It looks like the mountains over there," she said, pointing.

Paul put his hands on her shoulders. "That sounds like their creation mythology. Climbing out of a *kiva* in the earth, an underground ceremonial room. Can you ask him where he's from?"

Niki looked over her shoulder at Paul, thinning her lips at the suggestion. "I don't speak his language."

"Oh, right." Paul turned to the elder. "Do you recognize the language?"

The old man placed a finger beside his mouth. "Some of it sounds like my grandfather used to speak. The accents are different, but I think some of the words are the same."

"Can you ask him where he's from?" Paul asked.

The old man spoke something. The young man answered.

The old man's eyes widened, then he frowned. He repeated his question and the young man replied again. Speaking to Paul, the elder said, "He says they come from Sixth World."

Niki felt Paul's hands squeeze her shoulders, as if he were excited by what he heard. She asked, "What's that?"

The elder answered. "Our people believe we live in the Fifth World. Simply put, when this world can't support us any longer, we will be told to go to Sixth World."

The other elder jumped in and spoke angrily to the young guy. Niki looked to Anne for explanation.

"He's accusing the guy of making it up. Says they all know no one has gone to Sixth World yet. Fifth World will die when they leave it."

Niki shivered. She didn't care where the young guy came from. She didn't want to hear about her world dying.

One of the singers joined them. "What's this about?"

The first elder explained what was happening. The singer nodded and held out his hand to the stranger. "I'm Tom Miller. Is your band planning to stay a while?"

The young guy looked at Tom's hand, then shook it. He didn't speak.

Tom turned to the old man. "Dad, let's get back to the motor home."

Both of the elders followed Tom, leaving Paul, Niki and JC with the newcomers. JC nudged her. "We should go, too."

Niki wanted to hear more about where these people came from. She didn't have the same suspicions as the elders, but the story was crazy. Interesting crazy, not batshit. She thought back to Antwon's grin at being told he was crazy like they were. Niki had a feeling this new guy was a crazy mo-fo, too.

"Yeah, let's go." She wrapped her arm around JC and left the ceremonial circle.

Chapter Seventeen

Niki needed quiet.

The entire gathering buzzed about something that morning, and she wanted to cover her ears and scream for quiet. Since that wasn't what grown-ups do and she was trying so hard to continue to act like one, she wandered away from the campers and tents. She climbed the first hill she came to and stood at the peak, scanning the land where the meteor had hit.

Uncertain what she expected to see, she couldn't say she was disappointed that it looked...normal. Maybe she was too far away to see the crater. JC had said it was small, but nothing small could have made the ground shake the way it had.

She sat in the dirt. Anne appeared and sat beside her. "Hey," Anne said.

"Hey. So what's the story with those people last night?" Niki asked.

"He told you guys."

Niki frowned. "He came from another world? Yeah, right."

"Yeah, right. And you talk to dead people."

"Point taken. And Antwon can leap tall buildings in a single bound."

Anne laughed, the sound ringing in Niki's head, spreading light as it did.

Niki sighed. "I miss you."

Rolling her eyes, Anne said, "You see me almost every day."

"But you're not—" Niki caught herself as she realized what she was about to say.

"I'm not real? You just can't let go of that. The world is different now, but it's still real. You guys aren't the only ones suddenly discovering new talents."

"But I don't get it. Why can we do these things?"

"The question should be, why couldn't you do them before? You are the same people you were."

"What good is it if you answer my questions with questions? Don't you have access to stuff we don't, now that you're over there?"

"I like that, over there. Across the great divide." Anne straightened her legs and leaned back on her hands. "Do you really want to get into metaphysics? I can tell you about the thinning of the veil, the meaning of life, and all that, but would you believe it?"

"Believe it, or understand it? I did okay in school. I don't get why this is so hard for me to adjust to."

"Give it time, you'll get there." Anne turned toward the sound of footsteps, and Niki did, too. Where she hoped to see JC, instead she saw the new guy.

"Hey," she said.

He said something she didn't understand.

"Um, so did you guys get settled in last night? You looked good dancing." Niki looked at Anne, but didn't want to ask questions if the guy was only pretending he couldn't understand her.

Again, he spoke in the strange language, directing his words at Anne.

Anne responded in his language. Niki shook her head in amazement. "How do you know that language?"

"How do you not?" Anne laughed. "I'm kidding. What good would it be if we couldn't all speak the same language in the afterlife?"

"Wait, you mean, he's dead, too?"

"No, he's as alive as you are." Anne spoke to him again and he laughed. She turned back to Niki. "He's cute, isn't he?"

Niki nodded, praying he didn't understand English. Then it hit her. "He can see you?"

"He can. He thinks we dress funny."

Niki studied him. He wore white again, a pullover cotton shirt and pants tucked into knee-high moccasins. His belt was woven fiber. His hair was shoulder length, straight and black. He studied her while she checked him out, and she grew warm from being caught staring. She stood. "I'm Niki."

Anne translated for her. The guy answered, and Anne said, "His name is Wiago."

"So, where is he from?"

"He says the same as last night. Sixth World."

"But where is that? And is he crazy? Or making it up?" Niki couldn't blindly believe something so unlikely.

"It's not like people change color or something when they lie, Nik, but I see him living in a pueblo in a cave. Like in the olden days, before the Spanish settled out here."

"So he's either a blast from the past, or he really lives in a parallel time. It's so weird."

Anne spoke to Wiago and he laughed. She explained to Niki, "He thinks your world is pretty strange, too."

Niki didn't want to be alone with the guy, even if she had been able to see what he was thinking. Even with Anne acting as translator. He seemed normal enough, but what did they know about him? "Yeah, well. Tell him it was nice meeting him, but I have to go now. Bye."

~*~

JC watched Niki on the hilltop talking to the guy who arrived last night. Not just talking, laughing. Having a good ol' time. He crossed his arms over his chest. Just because the guy knew some native songs and dances didn't mean he could steal Niki from him.

She walked down the hill alone, waving when she saw JC. He lifted a hand, then shoved his fists in his pockets. He really wanted to punch the guy, which Niki wouldn't like.

When she reached JC, she smiled. "Hi. Whatcha doing?"

He grabbed her by the waist and pulled her roughly against him, bent his head and kissed her. He wanted to brand her with his lips. Not a love bite, but kiss her so hard any guy who looked at her would know she belonged to him.

Her arms snaked up around his shoulders. She moaned softly, her breath whispering on his cheek. His hand ran over her back, fitting her to him. When he realized they were in full few of anyone looking that way, he lifted his head, watching her eyes.

Niki blushed and smiled. "Miss me?"

"Yeah," he croaked. He cleared his throat with a laugh. "I was going to go out to the crater again. Want to come?"

"Yeah, sounds good."

~*~

When they returned to the campsite later that evening, they found Paul sitting with the elders, the newcomers and a few of the drummers. He motioned them over. "To borrow a phrase from Destinee, this is so cool! These people are Anasazi."

The word meant nothing to Niki. "Is that another tribe?"

"It's the name given to the Ancient Ones, who vanished before the Spanish came to the area."

"Where did they go?"

"To the next world. I studied different versions of the mythology before meeting Wiago. There were three worlds before the one we live in. Each tribe has its own variation of how the worlds were destroyed. But they all agree that as one world ended, the chosen ones were warned by the gods to go to the next world."

Niki tried to make sense of this. "But he was in the world after this one, and this world still exists." A wave of panic churned her stomach. Was he here to tell them their world was ending?

Paul smiled. "This is the part that's so cool. In the Sixth World there are people from all the tribes that existed at the time the Ancient Ones left. Not just the Puebloan people, but all the tribes on the continent, including those south of us, like the Mayans."

He seemed to be watching them for a reaction. And when Niki caught on, her jaw dropped. "The Mayans."

Nodding, Paul said, "Exactly. Wiago's story differs from the traditions I've read. The Ancient Ones were given a specific date, many years in the future, when the cleansing of the Fifth World would be complete, and they would be given a sign to return."

Niki glanced at the young native, and his friend behind him. "No way."

"Way." Paul nodded.

"What?" JC asked.

"Okay, some of the people who were told about Sixth World were Mayans, and they were given a date when it would be safe for them to return..." Niki watched JC to see if he understood.

"So they had a calendar showing the date..." he added. "December 21, 2012."

Antwon laughed. "Cool. But do you believe Wiago?"

Paul's mouth pulled to one side. "I'm trained to get several sources to confirm something before I treat it as fact. These people claim to be from one clan, and not the Mayans. So I am extrapolating here. Wiago says they followed the falling stars to this place, and a new sun opened the sky for them to climb the ladder back into this world."

JC nodded. "The stars led them here."

Paul smiled. "I thought you'd like that part."

Niki scanned the newcomers, easily recognizable in white. They reminded her of old black-and-white movies showing the Apache people. She wanted to believe their story. It was no more far-fetched than what she and the guys could do, if she admitted the truth.

One point had her praying it was true. If they'd been led to return to this world, it meant this world wasn't going away.

~*~

The dance that night was one of celebration. The elders were either convinced of the truth of the newcomers' tale, or wanted to move on in spite of the interruption. The non-native campers were more than happy for an excuse to party, and broke out some treasured beer and wine supplies.

One of the Anasazi women led Niki and Destinee through the steps of the women's dance. It was an easy shuffle, but Niki never claimed an ounce of coordination in her being. Once she stepped on her own toe and fell, giggling, against Wiago. He laughed, shaking his head and saying something.

Niki wished she could speak his language. She watched his face, waiting for the images to appear as they sometimes did when he talked. But none came.

The girl who'd been teaching her tugged on Niki's sleeve and motioned with her feet. Niki nodded, "Okay, I'll try again."

She watched her feet and the girl's feet, afraid to look up and trip again. When she finally felt her feet knew what they were doing, she braved a glance at the people around her. A few feet in front of her, JC's mom danced. She wore a bright yellow, straight dress that ended at her knees, and had a matching shawl draped over her arms. Long fringe fell from the shawl and the dress, accenting her moves when she twisted and turned.

Niki drew in a quick breath. His mom looked so beautiful, so happy. Niki needed to talk to JC right away. She turned abruptly and plowed right into Wiago. He caught her arms, shook his head with a smile and led her outside the dancing circle. He motioned toward the table where the punch cups were, but she shook her head.

She stood on her toes to see over the dancers but couldn't find JC. Placing her hand on Wiago's sleeve, she said, "Excuse me, I need to find my boyfriend."

Heading toward Lisa, Niki searched the crowd. Antwon stood with some guys they'd met since coming to the new lake. Paul spoke to an elderly couple. But JC was nowhere in sight.

A hand grabbed her from behind and Niki jumped, startled. She spun, and relaxed when she saw JC. "There you are."

"I was watching you dance with the new guy."

She rolled her eyes. *Don't be a dude, now, JC, this is important.* "If you were watching, you saw I wasn't dancing with him, and he caught me when I repeatedly tripped. But that doesn't matter. I have to tell you something."

His lips were thin, and he shoved his hands in his hoodie pockets. At least he didn't mess with his beanie and totally drive her nuts.

"Your mom is here again."

"Cool." His face and posture didn't agree with the word he used.

"It is cool. She's dressed like the dancers."

JC lifted one eye brow. "Oh, yeah?"

"Yeah. See the lady in the turquoise dress with all the fringe? Your mom's is like that, but yellow. She has her hair braided, too. She looks like she could be one of the dancers."

He grunted. "What's it mean?"

"I don't know. I mean, Anne could talk to Wiago in his own language, but she said they didn't have language barriers in the afterlife. Your mom might have wanted to dress up for the fun of the party. But the style suits her. Do you think she might have been Native American?"

JC watched the dancers for a bit before answering. "She never said."

Niki's excitement faded. "Oh."

"She didn't like to talk about the past."

"You felt like you were following the stars to come here." Niki hugged his arm. "Just like the Anasazi.

Wouldn't it be cool if your mom was descended from those Ancient Ones, just like these people?"

He didn't respond. Niki went back to watching the dancers. She didn't see his mom anymore. The idea that JC might be standing among his people, distant relatives as they might be, left her with an emptiness in the pit of her stomach. Lisa was like a mom to her, but Niki didn't think she'd ever feel whole again with Crystal gone.

Her eyes filled with tears. Desperate to get away before anyone saw her cry, she mumbled to JC, "I'm going to the campsite."

She hurried, stumbling blindly through the crowd that had to be twice as large as it was an hour earlier. People were coming from everywhere, practically crawling up out of the ground just outside the last line of campers. Not Anasazi. The license plates on their cars said they came from her world. There were just so many of them.

She couldn't find peace at her campsite, with neighboring sites filled with people talking and laughing. Niki continued outward, past the last of the campsites. No one was on the beach, so she went there.

She fell to her knees on the shore and let her sadness take over. Sobs tore through her, her eyes and nose running with tears. How long was it going to hurt like this? She needed to get over losing Crystal or she'd never be really happy.

"Hey, are you okay?"

Niki ran her coat sleeve over her face before lifting her head. A blonde girl stood in the dark a few feet away. "Yeah, I'm fine."

"Niki?"

Her head snapped up, recognizing the voice. She burst into a fresh round of tears realizing it was her sister's ghost beside her. "I miss you."

"I missed you, too." Crystal stepped closer and pulled Niki's hair back. "I was afraid you were dead."

"No, then I would have been able to find you."

"What do you mean?"

Niki looked up. "Like Anne comes to me all the time. Don't you just think of someone and you're there?" She wanted to ask, *and what took you so long to think of me,* but was too glad to finally see her sister.

"I don't know what you're talking about. Let's go back. Mom and Dad will be glad to see you." Crystal held out her hand.

Niki took it for balance as she stood. Then realized the hand was warm. She squeezed it tightly.

"Ouch! What are you doing?"

Niki's heart stopped. "You're...alive?"

"Of course I am." Her look said she thought Niki was insane.

"Oh my God. I thought—Sherry said you were dead."

Crystal gasped. "You saw Sherry? She's okay?"

JC walked up at that point. "Hey, Niki, you all right?"

Niki burst out laughing, which quickly turned into hysterical tears. JC wrapped himself around her and whispered shushing noises. Through her noisy sobs, Niki heard him speak again.

"Are you Crystal?"

"Yes. I'm her sister."

"I thought I recognized you. She thought you were dead."

"So I gathered. How long is she going to keep crying?"

Niki sucked in a deep breath, willing her voice to cooperate. "Quit talking about me like I'm not here."

Crystal put one hand on her hip and threw her weight to one side. "So, are you going to introduce me to your boyfriend?"

"Sorry. This is JC."

"How come you never told me about him?"

JC loosened his grip on Niki. "Okay, not cool. I'm here, too."

Niki rested her palm on JC's chest and looked up at him as the realization of all he meant to her threatened to overwhelm her into tears again. "JC's, well, he's the best thing that ever came into my life."

She felt his heart speed up. She smiled at him, hoping, even in the moonlight, he could see everything she felt.

Crystal sighed. "That's cool. Let's go find my parents. They'll be so happy to see you. And to meet JC."

The Farmers' campsite was half a mile from the lake, telling Niki just how many people had arrived in the past two days. She wasn't imagining the population growth.

Crystal ran ahead the last few feet to the motor home. "Mom, Dad, come see!"

The door on the side opened and Mr. Farmer came out, followed by his wife. "What is it?"

"I found Niki," Crystal shouted with excitement.

"Niki!" Mrs. Farmer looked like she was going to run to Niki, but hesitated. Niki didn't, breaking free of JC's arm and running to the woman.

Wrapped in the warm embrace, Niki wanted to stay put. She was safe there, as safe as in JC's arms. She lifted her head. "I thought you all died in the tidal wave."

Mr. Farmer rested a hand on her head. "It was close, but we got away just in time. Why don't you guys sit?" He motioned to a folding picnic table.

As she sat, Niki asked, "How come I never found your name on the survivor lists?"

"I don't know," Mrs. Farmer said. She sat opposite Niki and JC, in between Crystal and her husband. "Once we were able to find transportation, we went to Bakersfield. Some friends were out of the country, so we stayed at their house."

JC sat up straighter. "Where was that?"

Interrupting, Niki said, "By the way, this is JC. He's the one who dug me out of my apartment building when it collapsed."

"It's nice to meet you, JC. Thank you for looking out for Nicole," Mrs. Farmer said. "We stayed in the northeast, near the college. On Columbus."

Niki grinned up at JC. "She was right."

"Who was?" Crystal asked.

Watching JC's expression for permission, Niki spoke at his nod. "It's kind of a crazy story. We thought JC's sister was trying to tell us where you guys were."

Mrs. Farmer's brows drew together. "But how would she know?"

"She's dead. She talked to JC a few times after she died in the earthquake." Niki waited for their reaction, ready to leave if they said anything against JC. She clutched his hand on her lap.

Crystal exchanged a glance with her mom. "Oh, kind of like Mikey."

"Who's Mikey?" Niki asked.

"He was my big brother. He died as a baby, before we went to live with the Farmers."

"I—I didn't know." They hadn't mentioned another child when Niki was living with them, but she'd only been there three months. Three months spent talking back, ignoring rules and spreading her hate.

"Not long after you left us," Mrs. Farmer explained, "Crystal started talking to an invisible friend. I thought it was a defense mechanism, trying to adjust to you being gone."

Crystal tipped her head from side to side. "Nope. I was talking to a ghost."

Niki grinned. "Remind me to introduce you to my friend, Anne."

Mr. Farmer just shook his head. He asked JC, "Your sister told you we lived on Columbus Avenue?"

"No. She had to be a brat about it. She kept chanting rhymes about Columbus, Garces and Monterey. I spent a night driving around in those areas just hoping to find a clue."

Mr. Farmer nodded. "Oh, they were there. Not that you'd know it. I worked at San Joaquin Hospital near Garces Circle after we moved there. And my wife worked at the Head Start center on Monterey."

"Wow." Niki couldn't believe it.

JC laughed. "Kaylee is giggling like crazy in my head, since we finally figured it out."

Smiling, Mr. Farmer tossled Crystal's hair. "Sounds like a girl."

They continued to catch up, talking until Niki couldn't hide her yawn. Mrs. Farmer rose from the table. "We should turn in. I can't tell you how happy I am to find you safe, Nicole."

She walked with Niki and JC to the edge of the camp, giving Niki another long hug. "I still think of you as my daughter, you know. I tried to pretend you'd gone off to school."

Niki's eyes welled. "I was such a bitch."

"You were a scared, desperate child who didn't know how to cope with structure."

"It sounds way nicer how you say it, Mrs. Farmer."

Mrs. Farmer smiled. "I love you, Niki. And you'd make me feel so much better if you called me Mom."

"Thanks. I...I love you, too."

Chapter Eighteen

JC awoke early, just as the sun rose. They'd had another late night around the bonfire, so he guessed most of the people in the camp would sleep in. Grabbing his crossbow and arrows, he pushed the dirt bike out past the lake before starting it up. He hoped to ride out far enough to find some jack rabbits for dinner. With all the uncertainty about how long they would stay and where to go next, they needed to stretch their supplies as long as possible.

He scanned the desert for any signs of movement but saw none. He kept riding, kept looking, kept trying to keep his mind on hunting and not the new guy that Niki spent so much time talking to. Paul had said the story about Sixth World was a tribal myth, which meant it was no more real than Cupid.

Where had Wiago and his friends come from? And why would they make up a crazy story that only made sense to the few people who knew the old stories of the Pueblo tribes? It didn't make sense.

JC wasn't surprised when he reached the crater

instead of the rock mound he'd aimed for. Circling the depression on the dirt bike, he decided to stop and have a better look. He could easily disprove the story by proving the crater was solid, no holes for anyone to climb up through.

The pit was too deep to jump into and expect to get back out easily. That was one point in his favor. They couldn't have climbed out. Niki had said she saw a ladder in the vision Wiago showed her. There was nowhere they could have hidden a ladder nearby. They would have had to carry it to one of the rocky mounds or hills.

More reasons to disbelieve the story.

On the far side of the crater, JC noticed shadows in an odd formation on the wall. Much too regular to be a natural pattern. Lying on the lip of the pit, he reached down to feel what seemed to be notches carved into the dirt. They formed a sort of ladder. He wondered who would have done that. A scientist would have wanted to leave the crater undamaged. Kids would have found an easier way down, if they'd been exploring.

Regardless of whoever had done it, the carvings allowed JC to climb down. With his crossbow slung over his back, he descended into the crater. When there was about four feet of dirt wall above his head, he thought he should feel the bottom, but a sweep with his foot hit only air. He continued down.

And down. The morning shadows couldn't account for the growing darkness. He looked up, but there was only six feet or so of crater wall above him. Another two steps down. The crater closed in on him, as if he crawled through a narrow opening and not a big pit. His foot still found only air when he kicked out.

JC debated going farther, or return to the desert

floor. Curiosity held him captive. Where was he going, and what was in the hole?

Four more steps down and his head cleared the narrow passageway. He was in a dark space, a cave or a room, he couldn't tell. A voice in his head told him how stupid he was to continue. But how could he not, when he was dying to find out where he was?

Well, maybe not dying to find out. It would suck if he died, but he couldn't quit now. He wished he'd brought a flashlight, or even a lighter, but he hadn't expected to be exploring. Keeping his right hand on the wall he'd just climbed down, he stepped carefully toward his left, circling the space.

The wall ended in a large opening, a passageway. JC pulled his crossbow off his back, loaded it, and moved into the passage. He saw light at the end and slowed down as he entered it to look around. The passage opened on a cliff wall, some twenty feet above the canyon floor.

Where the hell was he?

Birds sang in the canyon, and JC could hear moving water nearby. He held up a hand to block the sun. Trees and bright bushes snaked through the canyon, where he assumed the creek ran. He didn't see any people or large animals, but didn't relax his grip on the crossbow.

The only way down was another ladder of carved footholds. He had to put his crossbow on his back to descend. His feet shook slightly in the toeholds, and he debated for a few seconds going back for Paul. But Paul's leg was still healing, so he couldn't make the climb. JC wasn't about to risk Niki's life, bringing her here when he had no idea what he'd find. And he didn't know Wiago well enough to trust him.

At the bottom of the ladder, JC quickly searched the

area for signs he wasn't alone, then rushed to the cover of the trees along the creek. The moving water masked any other sounds. Keeping an eye to the ground for paw prints or animal droppings, he stayed in the sheltering brush and made his way downstream.

The canyon turned and the creek followed. As JC rounded the bend, he stopped, holding his breath. A woman with a large pottery dish filled it at the water's edge. She wore white, like Wiago and his friends, and had black hair wound in Princess Leia buns on each side of her head. Had she come from the campground, too?

JC was afraid to move. He didn't want to startle her. Didn't need her thinking he would hurt her.

The woman picked up her pot and stood. Seeing JC, she screamed and dropped the pot, which shattered on a rock.

He held up a hand. "It's okay. I didn't mean to scare you. I'm, uh, lost. Is the campground nearby?"

She turned and ran.

JC didn't follow, for fear of getting even more lost. He didn't remember a canyon in this part of the Mojave Desert, much less a creek, so the smart thing would be to go back. He could get Antwon or even Wiago to come explore further.

Following the creek back, he again stayed within the trees for cover. When he saw the tunnel in the cliff wall, he broke cover and jogged for the carved ladder.

An arrow whispered past his head.

He flinched, telling himself he imagined it. Whoops and yells broke out behind him. Five or six guys, wearing white, were aiming arrows his way. He'd never make it up the ladder in time.

~*~

Niki woke from her nightmare, wrestling with the sleeping bag tangled around her. Even after opening her eyes, the vision remained. JC was being chased by the Anasazi through a canyon.

She scrubbed her hands over her face, hoping to clear her head. She was probably remembering his complaints from the night before about how everyone believed the crazy stories the new people told, without questioning the logic of a parallel world.

Her panic didn't go away. Nor did the vision of JC darting from tree to rock, trying to get a good sight of the men chasing him so he could aim his crossbow.

Where was JC?

Slipping her feet into her shoes, she left her tent and found Paul sipping coffee while listening to his CB. She called to him. "Have you seen JC?"

Paul shook his head. "He left early this morning on the dirt bike. Haven't seen him since."

She pursed her lips. There was no way of knowing which direction he'd gone.

"What's wrong?" Paul asked.

"A vision woke me. JC being chased by the Anasazi."

"That's odd. They're a peaceful group. Why would they chase him?"

"I don't know." She put her hand to her chest. Her heart raced. "Something is wrong. I need to find JC."

Paul got out of his truck and grabbed his crutch. "Let's go see the Anasazi."

They found the group of newcomers at their campsite, the men skinning squirrels and jack rabbits they'd killed, the women cooking something in pots near the fire.

Niki called out to Anne in her thoughts. "I need you to translate, please."

Wiago rose and came to them. Paul shook his hand and spoke in the language Niki hadn't caught on to yet. Wiago shook his head and spoke to the other men. They all grunted, and Wiago shook his head again.

"They didn't see him when they went out this morning," Paul said.

Niki looked around, frustrated. "Where's Anne when I need her? Can you ask Wiago if he knows of a canyon around here?"

Paul made some strange sounds, with the word canyon thrown in their midst.

Niki grew frustrated. She could do that much. If she could see what Wiago pictured when he talked, could Wiago do the same? It was worth a try. She reached for his wrist, holding it while she looked him in the eye. "Can you see what I'm seeing?"

He held her gaze, his eyebrows drawing together. When Niki pictured JC running through a creek, Wiago's eyes widened and he pulled his arm free.

Wiago turned to the men behind him, saying something as he motioned toward the desert. The men jumped up, grabbing their weapons.

"What's happening?" Paul asked Niki.

"I think Wiago recognized where JC is. I hope so."

Paul turned to leave. "I'll get my Explorer so we can get there faster."

When they'd convinced the Anasazi to get in the SUV, Wiago pointed toward the crater. Paul drove in that direction. Niki's stomach cramped and twisted, her fear was so bad. She was only getting flashes of the vision, and the blood she saw on JC's jeans didn't help any.

Wiago shouted when they reached the crater. He and his men jumped out before the Explorer even stopped. Niki followed, against Paul's wishes.

"Wait, you need to stay here," Paul yelled, hobbling on his crutch after them.

Niki glanced back. "I can't. I need to help JC."

The Anasazi disappeared one by one over the side of the crater, yet when Niki reached the edge, she didn't see where they'd gone. She noticed the footholds, and began to climb down.

"Niki, it's not safe for you to go." Paul's voice sounded frustrated, as if he knew she wasn't going to listen before he even said it.

"Then it's not safe for JC either. I can't let him die." She continued down into darkness, wondering what she'd gotten herself into this time.

Once inside the dark room, she followed the soft sounds of the men's moccasins on the dirt, which led her down a tunnel. The bright light that appeared was no comfort when she didn't know what was ahead. Where were they? And how had they climbed through the dirt?

So many questions ran through her thoughts but she had to hurry to keep up. As she ran toward the light, the last of the men was disappearing down another ladder outside the end of the tunnel. Niki turned around and climbed down quickly, not wanting the chance for her fear of heights to kick in. She didn't want to know how far she could fall.

Her feet hit dirt. She almost collapsed in relief. But she needed to find JC. She looked around to see where she was.

The men ran toward the trees to her right, so Niki followed. She was not at all comforted by the fact they had their bows drawn. In her visions, JC was being chased by men in white. Panic swept over her. Had she turned the vision into reality by bringing the Anasazi here?

But Wiago had known where to go from what he'd seen. This must be where they came from, or someplace they'd passed through on their way. It didn't matter. Only JC mattered.

Niki couldn't catch her breath, she'd run so hard after the men. She hadn't seen JC, or anyone other than Wiago's friends. She kept running.

Up ahead, shouts echoed off the canyon walls. Niki didn't recognize the voices. She ran toward the sound, breaking out of the trees. Wiago's men were waving and yelling at some others who were peering out from behind large rocks. Niki stopped, unable to decide if it was safe to approach.

One man behind a rock aimed an arrow in her direction and she dropped to the hard dirt. Why were they shooting at her?

The argument raged on in Wiago's language. She wondered if he knew those other men, and if so, why they didn't stop arguing.

Suddenly JC's voice called out, "Niki."

Footsteps came her way. She lifted her head to see JC running to her. She waved an arm. "No, get down, they'll shoot you."

Before she finished, an arrow caught him in the side. He dropped to the ground.

"JC!" Niki was at his side before she could think about getting up. He groaned and reached for the arrow. She pushed his hands away. "Don't. You'll make it worse."

Her tears fell on his shirt where the arrow stuck out,

just above his hip bone. She wiped her eyes and looked for Wiago, who ran up and knelt near JC.

Niki couldn't focus on Wiago's words or the men approaching. If she lost JC…she couldn't even bear to think it. "We need to get him back to camp and get him medical help."

Wiago didn't respond. He examined the wound and broke off the arrow shaft a few inches from JC's skin. JC cried out when the arrow snapped. Motioning to his men, Wiago stood. They gathered around JC and lifted him, carrying him back the way they'd come.

Niki realized some of the men who'd been shooting at her and JC were now carrying him. She batted at their arms. "No, stop. Put him down."

JC moaned, then said, "It's okay, Mouse. I don't think they're going to hurt me."

"What do you mean, they already did." She swiped her sleeve across her face again.

"Wiago won't let them hurt me."

She wanted to trust, but it wasn't easy.

They carried JC to a place below a large cave in the canyon wall and set him down. Niki rushed to hold his head when the men stepped aside. Wiago handed her JC's crossbow and said something she couldn't understand. Once again, she wished Anne would appear and translate for them.

The Anasazi climbed another foothold ladder and disappeared into the large cave. Looking up at it, Niki realized it was the one she'd seen in her early visions, with pueblos inside the cave. The one she'd stood inside in her vision, when she'd looked out at the surrounding canyon. They had come to Wiago's home.

With the others gone, she stroked JC's hair and realized he'd lost his beanie cap. "How did you get here?"

"Same way you did, I guess. I climbed down the footholds in the crater."

"But why?"

"I wanted to know where they went."

She wanted to shake some sense into him. "But why did you go alone?"

A tear dropped on his forehead and she sat back on her heels. "Sorry. I sound like a mom, don't I?"

"It's okay. How did you know where I was? I thought I was going to die and you guys wouldn't even find my body."

"I had a nightmare that didn't go away when I woke up. I got Paul and he got Wiago. Luckily Wiago could see what I saw, and he led us here."

JC moaned and shifted his position. "This isn't gonna make me like the guy."

Niki shook her head. "I don't get why you don't like him."

Before JC could answer, Wiago returned with a gray-haired man who knelt beside JC. The old man tore open JC's shirt. Niki got lightheaded when she saw the arrow poking from his skin. She had to look away while the old man worked.

Finally, they sat JC up and wrapped a bandage around his middle. Wiago held out a hand to pull him to his feet.

Niki stood. She forced a smile for the old man. "Thank you."

He said nothing and returned to the cave.

Wiago motioned toward the ladder, speaking to JC and Niki. She looked at JC's injury, saying, "I think he wants us to go up. Can you climb?"

"I guess we'll find out. You go in front of me, so if I fall, I don't take you with me."

She hoped he was joking, and she was ready to make him stay on the canyon floor, except the only way back to their camp was by climbing the other ladder in the wall. Better to find out now if he could make it.

The pueblo sat toward the back of the cave. Other than the shelter above them, they could have been townhouses built anywhere in the southwest. No glass in the windows, and no fake lawns, but otherwise the same.

As they followed Wiago, Niki noticed the women staring at her and whispering. They wore white dresses, so her jeans must really look odd to them. Her hair hanging free, instead of being braided or rolled into buns, also stood out. Still, it felt like high school. Once again she was on the outside of the in crowd.

She chewed the inside of her cheek. This was life, not high school. She really needed to get over herself.

JC whispered to her. "I wonder where he's taking us."

"I don't know."

"Can't you read his mind?"

"No. That's not what we're doing, I don't think. We see each other's visions. Pictures, not words."

"Whatever. So, picture where he's taking us."

Before she could argue, Wiago climbed a ladder to the roof of the building and signaled for them to follow. An opening in the roof allowed them to climb down into the room. Niki wasn't sure what to expect, but was surprised to see only bright, woven blankets on the floor in the corner, with no furniture in the room. Wiago sat on one blanket and motioned to the others, where Niki and JC sat.

A woman came out of the adjoining room. Her eyes widened when her gaze met Niki's then she looked away. After Wiago spoke, the woman returned to the other room. She came back moments later with some small bowls, which she offered to the three.

Niki took a sip after seeing Wiago do so. The tea was somewhat bitter, and weaker than she was used to drinking. She smiled and nodded her thanks to Wiago.

Voices came from the roof and two older men entered. They sat near Wiago, who motioned toward first JC, then Niki, as if introducing them to the men. Niki waited, wishing she knew what was being said.

Suddenly she pictured the crater and campsite and she realized Wiago was telling them men where he'd been. A little girl came down the ladder and almost flew to Wiago, wrapping herself around him. He laughed, said something, then pointed to the ladder. The girl pouted, then left.

Feeling quite left out of the conversation, Niki watched the Anasazi speak to each other for at least an hour, then Wiago rose. He motioned to Niki and JC, who also stood.

Wiago led them back up the ladder to the outside, and down the ladder to the cave floor. The other men who'd come with them that morning sat nearby and rolled to their feet. Motioning for everyone to follow, Wiago led the way out of the cave.

~*~

JC climbed out of the crater and crawled on his knees, his side throbbing in pain. Niki climbed up behind him, then Wiago, who helped JC stand.

Paul sat inside his truck with his microphone in his hand. He jumped out and ran to them without his crutch. "Where the hell have you guys been?"

"Sixth World," Niki said simply, pulling JC's arm

over her shoulder.

"What?" Paul asked. "And what happened to you, JC?"

"Long story," JC said. Exhaustion made it difficult to think, much less speak.

The other men climbed up one by one. Paul pointed to the truck and everyone climbed in. No one spoke as they drove back to the campsite.

When they exited the Explorer, Wiago and his men went back to their camp. Niki helped JC to their tent with Paul following close behind.

Lisa rushed out of the pop-up trailer. "What happened? Where have you been?"

Paul put a hand on her arm. "We're about to find out. Let's let the man lie down."

Niki straightened the sleeping bags and folded one to use as a pillow, then helped JC lie down. Her forehead was wrinkled with worry. "Do you need some water? Are you hungry?"

"Not hungry, but I could use some ibuprophen." He sighed as he settled onto the floor of the tent. He was so tired he could sleep for a week.

"Niki, bring the first aid kit. It looks like you'll need it for changing his bandages over the next few days," Lisa said.

Glaring at JC from the corner of her eye, Niki said, "Don't start till I get back."

JC closed his eyes as he lay on the sleeping bags. He hated having to admit to dumbass moves, and this had to be the dumbest he'd done in a long time. He would have been killed if Wiago hadn't called off those men. He was lucky it was Wiago's people who were chasing him.

Paul and Lisa didn't get mad at him for going, and

didn't make him feel worse than he already did. He was afraid what Niki might have to say later, when they were alone. But he'd take whatever anger she shoved at him. He deserved it. And he was glad to be alive to hear it.

They had proved the existence of Sixth World. There was no other way to explain where they'd been. The canyon they'd been in wasn't on the map of the Mojave Desert, and it was much too large to be missed by surveyors and satellite cameras, both.

JC couldn't say exactly where Sixth World was, but he knew it was real. The old myths had been telling the truth.

Chapter Nineteen

After the meteorite strike, the earthquakes had ended. JC didn't see any more asteroids on his nightly search of the sky. Paul said the majority of the reports on the CB radio were of recovery, not more loss.

While the signs were all good, JC wondered what they were supposed to do next. At least while working at Oxy they'd had a goal. They were part of the recovery and had an option of housing coming in the near future. Here, they were biding time.

He and Antwon sat with Paul, Mr. Farmer and Wiago at the Farmers' campsite. JC wasn't sure he liked having Wiago with them, even if he had saved JC. The guy could only barely communicate with Paul, and spent way too much time with Niki, who seemed to understand him completely thanks to their shared visions.

JC would be perfectly happy if the Anasazi moved on, taking their leader, Wiago, with them. Or went back to Sixth World, now that they knew for sure it existed. He'd seen no sign Sixth World was dying when he'd been there, so there was no reason for them to remain here.

Only when he reminded himself the Anasazi had

been following the stars did he feel guilty for his attitude toward them.

"What's this Crystal mentioned about the coast?" Mr. Farmer asked Paul.

"There's a new city in the planning stages. It will be just east of what was Paso Robles."

"Sort of like Phoenix, rising from the ashes." Mr. Farmer stroked his chin. "It might be too confusing to call it Phoenix, though."

"It's not official, but the name they're using right now is Apocalyptia."

"That's a mouthful."

Paul nodded. "They want to change how people are using the word apocalypse, since that's what everyone is calling the changes we've gone through. Everyone took it to mean the end of days, but the biblical sense was that it was the final battle between good and evil. And good would triumph over evil. I'm sure it's some politician behind the naming. He'll probably run for president on a campaign of hope."

JC grunted. "Is hope a bad thing?"

"Not at all." Paul steepled his fingers, his elbows resting on the table, which JC recognized as the beginning of a lecture. "I think most of the people who survived will tell you hope is what got them through. They might call it faith, which I think is a stronger belief. But since most cities are rebuilding with knowledge being the only resource they've stockpiled, I think we're all going to need a lot of hope or faith in the coming days."

"Well put," said Mr. Farmer.

JC braced an arm on the table. "Are you planning to move to Apocalyptia?"

Twisting to face JC, Paul asked, "What are your

feelings about it?"

"I don't know. I just now heard of it."

"You know I value your input, JC. I plan for us to stick together no matter where we end up. And I won't make a decision to go anywhere without discussing it with you first."

JC nodded. Some of the pressure on his chest lifted. "We do need to go somewhere. There's nothing here for us to live on."

"You're right," said Mr. Farmer. "This new city sounds promising. There will be work for all of us. Schools. A new beginning."

Paul spoke to Wiago in the broken language they'd developed between them. After Wiago's reply, Paul told the others, "He says they need a place with good hunting, fresh water and good land for crops. He's hoping the stars will continue to lead them."

"They're just gonna farm?" Antwon asked.

"That will be interesting to find out, the longer they're here. I have a feeling they'll assimilate like their distant cousins who remained here in the Fifth World. There aren't enough of them to sustain a lasting society." Paul looked sad when he said this.

For a moment, JC wondered what it would have been like to live in the time before technology appeared. Thinking on their first days at the lake, he decided that was as close as he wanted to come to trying it.

~*~

Niki, Crystal and Anne walked together on the lake shore. Niki had been delighted to find out her sister could see and hear Anne. Their relationship was changing, too. Maybe it was because Niki could accept that the Farmers really cared about them. Crystal was four years younger than she, but Niki no longer felt like she had to be the boss. She could just be a sister now.

"I think it's crazy that Wiago can see you," Crystal told Anne.

"Why? You both do."

"I know. But he's a guy. And he's not from here."

"And he's so cute, isn't he?" Anne laughed. "He almost makes me wish I was alive again."

Niki looked at her in shock. "What do you mean, almost? You don't wish you hadn't died?"

Anne shook her head. "I don't feel like I left anything unfinished. I don't have all the angst I did when I was alive. Everything is so peaceful now."

Crystal shook her head. "You're *not* going to convince me I'd be better off dead."

"No. Not at all. Never think it!" Anne walked backwards, facing the sisters. "I died when I was supposed to. I have no idea what happens to people who die too soon. Maybe that's what hell is, living in eternal regret."

Niki scrunched her nose. "Do we have to talk about dying? I'd rather talk about living."

"Well, yeah." Crystal shoved Niki. "You have a boyfriend. Of course you do."

"Even if I didn't, I don't want to talk about death. That was all I thought about when I was buried in my apartment. What I really want is to get back to normal life. I want a job again. A reason to get up in the morning."

"And kissing JC isn't enough reason?" Crystal giggled.

Niki rolled her eyes. "I'm serious. I hope we figure out where to go from here, and soon."

As they neared the campsites, Mrs. Farmer saw

them and waved. They joined her and Lisa in walking to the Farmers' motor home.

"Did you two have a nice walk?" she asked.

"You three, you mean. Anne is here, too." Crystal pointed to their dead friend.

"I will never get used to this," Mrs. Farmer said.

"Tell her it's all right," Anne said. "She won't hurt my feelings."

The men sat at the table by the motor home. Niki walked over to JC and put her hand on his shoulder, standing behind him. Mrs. Farmer offered to refresh the coffee pot.

Mr. Farmer covered his mug with his hand. "We're fine, thanks, hon'. We're discussing the future."

"That sounds ominous. Any plans?" Mrs. Farmer reminded Niki of a housewife on TV. Not on one of those County shows, but on a sitcom. Neat, nurturing, together. Niki was certain no matter how long she practiced, she would never be so welcoming.

Paul spoke first. "Nothing even close to a decision yet. We need to find all our options and then we can make a sound choice."

Mrs. Farmer walked over to Antwon. "I'm told you left your family behind in Bakersfield."

"Yes, ma'am. My auntie and uncle had enough to worry about with their own kids."

"Well, if you find that living on your own isn't all it's cracked up to be, you are always welcome to stay with us."

Niki smiled. She knew the Farmers planned to stay with their group, but seeing Mrs. Farmer opening the door to Antwon made Niki love her even more.

Her eyes widened. She did love the Farmers, in spite of how hard she fought to escape their home. She knew the open door applied to her, too, should she ever want to come home.

Home.

There was that word again. Her stomach clenched and her bones ached just thinking about it. She nudged JC's shoulder. "Are you about done here?"

"Yeah, sure." He stood and they said their good-byes.

Niki led him toward their tent, holding his hand like a lifeline. Once inside the tent, she sank onto her sleeping bag, sitting cross-legged.

JC sat facing her. "What's up?"

"I was getting overwhelmed."

"Can I help?"

"You help just by being here," she said. "I want so badly to have walls, a door, running water. I want a real home."

The line between his brows disappeared.

"I am such an awful person." She chewed her lip.

His eyes narrowed, but he didn't give her that here-we-go-again look.

"I know I keep saying it, but I want to be sure I never act that way again. The Farmers love me. I treated them horribly and they still love me. Lisa and Paul love me, too."

"You never ran away from Lisa and Paul."

"No, I didn't. And I didn't run away from you."

"But, you wanted to."

She blinked rapidly when her eyes filled with those blasted girl-tears again. "But I wanted to. Only at first. I didn't know what to do with you. You didn't make fun of me, or try to feel me up—"

"But I wanted to."

Niki laughed and rolled onto her hands and knees,

crawling to him. "I don't know what I did to deserve you, but whatever it is, I want to keep on doing it."

He leaned his forehead against hers. "I don't know why I never tried to talk to you. I almost missed out."

"I love you, JC Phillips."

"I love you, too, Mouse."

She snorted. "You'd better kiss me damn good to make up for that, Mr. Phillips."

Cupping the back of her head, JC did just what she asked.

If you enjoyed Niki and JC's journey, watch for the next book in the Apocalyptia series coming Summer of 2013.

CHOSEN

The outcast. Her boyfriend. A ghost. And a guy from an ancient world. These are the chosen ones?

JC thought once they moved to Apocalyptia life would get easier. They have jobs and homes, and the Changes are a thing of the past. But Niki is spending way too much time with the new guy while JC is fighting the outsiders who are threatening the safety of the new city.

There are times when JC would gladly give back any gifts he was chosen to receive. Especially when those gifts are driving him and Niki apart.

Dear Reader:

This book is fiction, but Wiago's world is based on fact. Blended histories, to be exact. Many of the Southwestern US and Mexican native people believe the world we currently inhabit is the Fifth World (Fourth, for the Hopi). They have individual legends about how each world was destroyed, leading their ancestors to move to the next. I combined the beliefs in creating my version the Anasazi, mostly out of respect. While I have some Native American ancestry, it's so far back I had no access to the old stories as I grew up. Stories get told and retold and drift a bit from the original, so I don't like to rely on what I read as fact. And fiction allows me to play with reality, as I did with the meaning of the date on the Mayan calendar.

The sad truth is, as we assimilate and stop being Irish-American, Black-American, Japanese-American or whatever blends you have in your background, we lose the traditions and stories of our ancestry. I encourage everyone to find out what you can about where your family came from. History becomes rich and, yes, interesting, when you realize your great-great-grandfather saw it happen. And if, like JC, you don't know where your family came from, find some traditions that sing to your soul and embrace them as your own.

I wish you happy reading in your quest to find your past. And I hope you'll join me again for my twisted version of reality.

Yours in reading,

Aileen Fish

About the Author

Aileen Fish is a multi-published author under several pen names, with stories ranging from historical to paranormal, or both, and heat levels from sweet to scorching. She is also an avid quilter and auto racing fan who finds there aren't enough hours in a day/week/ lifetime to stay up with her "to do" list. There is always another quilt or story begging to steal away attention from the others. When she has a spare moment she enjoys spending time with her two daughters and their families.

Stay up to date with book releases at her website http://aileenfish.com or on Facebook

Do you like your romance steamier? Check out http://arithatcher.com!

Other Books by Aileen Fish

Buy links are available at http://aileenfish.com/ books.html

Paranormal Romance
Immortal Temptress
Renegade Wolf
The Lives of Jon McCracken (print and ebook)

Regency Historical Romance
The Christmas Wedding Scheme
The Mistletoe Mishap
The Viscount's Sweet Temptation (In A Summons from Yorkshire anthology)
His Impassioned Proposal
A Christmas Courtship

Urban Fantasy
Outcast
Contemporary Romance
A Grand Beginning (In Love Everlasting anthology)
Passings in the Night (In Love Everlasting anthology)

www.ingramcontent.com/pod-product-compliance
Lightning Source LLC
Chambersburg PA
CBHW030303180626
46810CB00003B/899